I can lie here and hope the police save me and save them, or I can do something myself, and maybe help someone and maybe save a life.

**And maybe lose mine.**

**Survival is all that counts.**

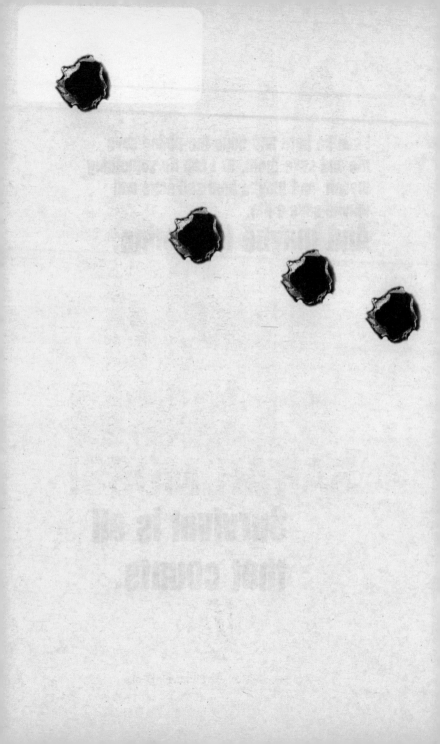

# SIEGE

## SARAH MUSSI

*Hodder
Children's
Books*

A division of Hachette Children's Books

For my mother and Minty,
who liked this best.

'If you leave this story feeling
unsettled,
disturbed,
alarmed that this could happen–
**good.**
You should be alarmed.
That is the point:
**to scare you,**
to make you not want to be
another
mindless,
thoughtless
follower.'

Adapted from Harry Knowles,
Ain't It Cool News

*In the time before the shooting I was Leah Jackson, sixteen years old. I used to wish my life was different. I had one brother of thirteen, Connor; one six-year-old sister, Sally. No dad. Not one I'd ever met, anyway. A mum with depression.*

*In the before time, I took care of everyone.*

*It was quite simple.*

*If I didn't take care of them I wouldn't have a family.*

*Neither would Sally, nor Connor.*

*But nothing is ever that simple, is it?*

# 9.22 a.m.
## Friday, 18 September

The windows start rattling. They're small, thick things, made of cheap blast-proof plastic, suitable for our kind of school. They mask another sound, something like popcorn popping. I tilt my head, trying to make it out.

It's coming from the gym, from morning assembly. Must be some surprise show for Own Clothes Day. Something like a cheer goes up; people start screaming, chairs scraping, fireworks firing. They're having fun. I stare at the ceiling. If it hadn't been for stupid Connor I'd be in there enjoying myself.

I fix my gaze on the ceiling tiles. The rattling stops. I can still hear humming. That means Lock Down is still on. I stay tense. Miss Carter's going to pick on someone now. Rub it in. *See what you miss when you're late for school.* The rattling starts again. A sharper, crisper, popping noise. Another bout of screaming. Louder, or am I listening harder?

Then there's a crash, like a door slamming, the patter

5

of feet, like someone's sprinting. That don't sound right even to me.

Two benches away my mate Kady looks up.

I chew my lip. Miss Carter is still looking to pick on someone. She already sent Tariq to the Head's office. Could be anyone next. Although if she's sent him, she mightn't want to send another; might look like she can't cope. But sprinting in the corridors. Someone's gonna get it for sure.

Another crackling sound and definitely running. I cross my fingers under the bench. Miss Carter don't care if you ain't done nothing. She'll pick on you just the same. Please don't let it be me.

Miss Carter screws up her face, spins on her heel and marches towards the door. She snorts as she moves. She's going for the source. Good. I flex my ankles, breathe out slowly, uncross my fingers.

Before she makes it to the door some kids bust in. Two of them. No polite knock. No note. No uncertain hovering.

I half rise, alarmed. Now we're *all* going to get it. My head starts banging. That's so unfair. They're so stupid. They walk right up to Miss Carter. They crazy? She opens her mouth in a snarl. She ain't seen such rudeness since Psycho Sam.

There's something about the way they do it. With no fear. Even Psycho Sam picked his battles. Suddenly I'm on automatic. I ain't seen kids act like this before. Something's up. I start backing up towards the tech den door. I'm out my seat. Am I crazy too?

I can't help it. Something ain't right.

I crouch, ready for anything.

One of the kids pulls out something. He's smiling. My mouth drops slack. Looks like a gun. Can't be. It's realistic though. He's gone loop. Must have. He's *so* going to be on the Volunteers' Programme next week. It happens, you know. It's not just a rumour. The End of Your Education. You Are Now Officially Slave Labour. He shoves the gun at Miss Carter. Must be one of those copy weapons they sell everywhere.

It's not.

And then there's this noise and this hole appears in Miss Carter's forehead. A small, red, round hole. It's got delicate edges that unfold like rose petals. She's grunting like some kind of tribal pig. Then I see the blood and her eyes and her mouth starting to sag open, and it's all gone mad. And the kid is wheeling round with an impossible grin on his face, waving the gun at us. And somebody is screaming. They're all screaming. Except me.

For one mad second I think they've come to liberate

us. Do Away With Teachers. Do Away With Detentions. But I'm wrong. The boys' eyes tell me. I can't make out who they are. I'm so shocked I can't make out anything. They're out of school uniform; could be anyone. Don't stare at them, Leah. Don't make a sound. I'm too shocked to make a sound. School uniform makes you a school kid. Those two ain't school kids no more. They've bust loose. They don't care about students versus teachers. They've fricking bust loose. They don't care about nothing. They're just doing destruction. One of them is kicking over the teacher's stool. Aliesha's screaming, Kady's screaming, all the kids in detention are screaming.

I see Anton moving for the door to the tech den. I back up further. I forget about Kady and Aliesha and the screaming others. I'm going to follow Anton. Kady's a drama queen and Aliesha's a loser, but Anton's smart. I like him. He likes me. And what good will it do staying with Kady and Aliesha?

The first killer seems unsure whether to fire at me. Instead, he raises his gun. He points it at Aliesha. He swings it towards Kady. They're both screaming. He likes the screaming. He says, 'Eeny meeny miney mo. We are the Eternal Knights.' And then he shoots Aliesha. She falls. He carries on shooting.

I'm almost at the door to the tech den. Almost through

it. Anton is nearly there too. I look at Anton. I'm thinking: *Get out. Hide. Get out. Hide. Get out. Hide.*

Suddenly Anton is right beside me. 'Run,' he hisses.

I leap from the lab, burst through the tech door, don't bother with no one else; I'm into that tech den like a bullet. I pull at chairs and bins and leap the benches. Vials and shit crash to the floor. I tear through it, swerve shelves, rip through air like it's got a sell-by date.

Footsteps crash behind me. Them? Kady? Did she get out? Not her. Must be Anton. Clever Anton. He's in Year Ten, different, not really Challenge School material. It better fricking well be Anton.

I can hear ragged breath right at my back. Someone's bellowing. And getting closer. Up ahead is Lab Two. When I reach it, I see it's empty. Ten metres empty. I weave in between the lab benches, ducking, leaping, twisting. How good a shot can those kids be? The floor's covered with smooth plastic tiling. Treacherous. If I slip, I'll crash. A booming, popping, shrieking tears past me. Christ, they're shooting at me!

Holy shit! My only chance is to get across the lab. I topple a pile of books, kick over the apps systems. My lungs can't make it. I got one chance. On the other side of Lab Two is the Level A corridor, but down some stairs, round a corner, past office doors and toilets, the

Level B corridor leads to the Humanities wing and the side entrance.

One chance.

Get to the exit. Challenge Schools are built on the transparency system. It's going to be impossible. They call it the Nowhere To Hide build. But that's them. We call it the Know Where To Hide. But do I? And even if I know somewhere, they will too.

Just run.

Just pray.

Just make it to the side entrance.

Is Aliesha dead? If not, she needs help. She always needs help.

Is Kady dead?

Go back?

Out. Of. The. Question.

This is it then.

There's a deafening roar behind me. They're into Lab Two, only ten, fifteen metres behind me.

I run.

Just before the steps to Level B, I sprint, stopping at the turn of Level A; I take the stairs. I'm in the air. I scream, my arms outstretched in front of me. I hit the ground still running and tumble forward. Keep running.

I turn towards the toilets.

# 9.30 a.m.
## Friday, 18 September

People sometimes ask you what you'd do in an emergency, like there's time to plan. You can't plan. You don't think. You just do something. It's like there's this thing in you that kicks in and you're on automatic. Action that comes straight from the brain and the character and experience.

I turn to the toilets.

I whirl. I see the kids reflected in the Level B windows of The Crossing. Think of a mall or a prison. Levels in tiers of glass from a central, open-to-the-roof highway: The Crossing. Level A (floor one), Level B (ground floor), Level C (lower floor), four wings L, M, N, O – shaped like an H.

There's a pounding behind me. Very Close.

I shrink into the toilet alcove.

It's Anton.

'Humanities!' I hiss at Anton.

There's a sudden scream cut short from somewhere.

11

Anton and I race out into the Humanities corridor. There's the exit at the end of it. Run for the exit. Someone else is running for the exit. They pull at the door. They can't get out. Then I realise it's Total Lock Down.

Total. Fricking. Lock. Down.

Not your poxy lie-on-the-floor-till-the-bells-go Lock Down, neither. I'm talking the full Secure and Seal System devised since the last lot of riots when kids thought it'd be fun to nick all the computers and burn down the schools. I'm talking: metal door grilles, steel window blinds, smoke-sensitive water sprinklers, perimeter-fencing electrocution, high-voltage fields on every side of the building. Lock Down that the police can initiate from the safety of their little Lock Downed stations.

The kid at the exit is screaming and screaming. He's tugging on the fire bar, but it's not opening the doors. He don't know you've got to have the fire alarms going to open the doors during Total Lock Down. The fire alarms'll only go if they sense massive carbon dioxide or something on the *inside*. Carbon Dioxide Activators are another new system the government's designed to Keep Kids Safe. Aka: Stop kids escaping. Stop kids setting off the fire alarms for fun. Like that's fun even.

I think he's a kid called Theo, in Year Eight. He's always out of class, roaming. His screaming draws the killers. I hear them dropping down the staircase I just jumped from. They're squealing in glee and racing out of the stairwell behind us. Hide. Forget exits. Forget Theo. Desperate, I search around. Lockers. Thank God for fricking lockers. I duck into a space behind the lockers. My heart's pounding fit to bust. Anton's too. He ducks in with me. Anton smells of fresh laundry. The two boys race past. I watch. Holding my breath. Heart exploding. They reach Theo. One of them says, 'Any last words for Mummy?'

Theo is crying, begging, screeching. One of them says, 'We are the Eternal Knights.'

I don't wait to hear it. I nudge Anton and we make a run the other way. While I'm running, I hear shooting. I imagine the blood splatter on the exit door that didn't open.

Theo, the little kid who liked to be free.

The corridors are empty now. Everyone's in assembly, aren't they? That's where it started. Didn't it? We must have been the only ones to escape. Except the new Year Sevens. They have their own assembly in the library. Did the killers go there first, before the Detention Lab? There's no way out. And the library runs the entire length of The Crossing on Level B. No way past it. Get to the library then. If they're all dead in there? Lie down too;

play dead. If they're not? They can't kill everyone. They'll run out of bullets. Hide at the back. I'll never make it. Everywhere's on Lock Down. Even the toilets. I stop. I swerve. I nearly bash into Anton. I head back down the Humanities corridor to the library.

Hide with the Year Sevens.

Dead or alive.

# 9.37 a.m.
## Friday, 18 September

They're alive.

Inside the library I run. The Deputy Head, Miss Turnbull, is taking the Year Seven assembly. Miss Cook, the Head, must be out of school today. Lucky. She says to me, 'Stop that immediately!'

I scream at her. 'They killed Miss Carter!'

There must be some power in my voice. I can see the Deputy Head believes me.

'Hide,' yells Anton, and there's something in his face and his speed that gets everyone scattering. The Year Sevens start screaming. I try to say, 'Don't scream. They'll hear.' But nobody listens. Some kids are running and shoving each other out of spaces under tables, under computers, behind book screens. I stand there. My brain is saying: *Run. Hide. Run. Hide.* But there's nowhere to hide.

'The ceiling. Help me,' hisses Anton.

He shunts a table. I drag a chair up on to it. I jump on that. It's nowhere near tall enough. Anton shunts another

15

table closer. There's a lot of screaming. This is madness. I want to scream too. But my voice is on mute. Hide in the ceiling. I kick the chair off. I help Anton put a table on a table, and I don't even know how I just managed to do that. He passes the chair back up. One little Year Seven sees what I'm doing. She's a kid called Ruby. I know her. She went to Daisy Bank Primary. She was nice to Sally when all the other kids weren't. She's smart and busy. Anyway she comes close. And soon there are three of us trying to build a tower to the ceiling tiles. I'm up on the tables and up on the chair. And I'm there.

I remove the ceiling tile and above is a gap. Some debris falls into my eye. I swear, rub my eye. Is this how I'm going to die? Because some dust got in my eye? I can't see where to push myself to. But I push myself anyway. The effort of pushing wobbles the chair, and the table shudders. I'm in the ceiling. The chair crashes down. I jolt, because for a minute I think the crashing is gunfire. I think it's them, already in the library. The gunmen are here. But they're not gunmen, are they? They're only boys, Year Nine boys, just like Connor. Where is Connor? It's not them anyway. Maybe they won't come. I roll into the ceiling. I remember I mustn't put weight on the polystyrene tiles. If the tiles break, those Year Nine boys will see me. So I drag myself with my arms across the ceiling slats, dislodging a tile as I go. The tile flips up and I can see down.

I can see Ruby, the little Year Seven; she's up on the chair, up on the two tables already. She's trying to get into the ceiling, but she's too short. Anton pulls her off and pushes past. It's Anton who's getting up on the tables now. He's taller, so he can reach up and do it.

For a minute I think he's going to lift little Ruby up. I don't know how I feel about that. A Year Seven kid might squeal, like Theo did. A Year Seven kid might break a polystyrene tile. But it's Ruby, the little girl with the pony tail who stuck up for Sally. I want to help her. But when Anton shoves her aside and stamps on her hand so she lets go, I'm glad too. I'm horrified that I'm so glad.

There is no time to think about it. Anton heaves himself into the roof. As he does this he deliberately kicks the tables and chairs down. They go crashing to the floor. That's good. No clue to show we climbed up.

Anton's lying flat on the joists. He looks at me. His eyes are empty. He just kicked a Year Seven kid out of the way to save his own skin. A kid we should have protected. And I'm glad. I can't bear how glad I feel. But Anton is years ahead of her in experience. He's just survived the last fifteen minutes. He knows what we're

17

up against. Anton is not going to squeal and give me away.

Anton lays a finger across his lips, rolls over and replaces the ceiling tile. I realise the tile I knocked is still crooked. So I very carefully inch round. I pick the tile clear of its joists. I'm terrified I'm going to drop it. My hands are shaking. Through the gap, before I put the tile back, I see Ruby. She's nursing her hand. She's trying to crawl under a computer desk, but they're all taken. She looks up at me, tears rolling down her face. She's clutching a little gold cross around her neck. Clutching and un-clutching it, with her bad hand all nursed up against her tiny chest. Her eyes are saying, Help me. Her eyes are wide, just like Sally's. I point to the book cupboard. I try to tell her the touch pad code by holding up my fingers, but there's no time, and anyway she ain't got the key. I point to the quiet corner where the beanbags are. She understands. She crawls there and pulls a beanbag over her. I put the ceiling tile back. I realise I've put it back wrong. It don't slot into place. There's a crack.

I pray that Ruby won't get hurt. I pray she won't tell where I am. I pray the killers won't look up at the ceiling. I pray if they do look up at the ceiling, they won't notice one of the tiles ain't straight. I pray if they do notice one of the tiles ain't straight, they won't think it's because

18

someone is hiding up here.

I pray and pray. Don't let them start shooting into the ceiling.

And I lie there, too scared to remove the tile and replace it properly. I'm frozen on the thin ceiling. Like on a web of ice. One wrong move. I can't bear to think about it. I'm scared I'll knock something and give us away. I'm trembling. I can't stop trembling. I'll tremble so much the tiles will crack and break and I'll fall through. Back into the library. I'm sweating. It's all slippery. I'm going to slip. It's dark; I'm going to fall. I must control my breathing. I must.

I must control my breathing.

Have to.

I have to look through the crack in the ceiling. I have to see what happens. I tell myself it's because I need to phone for help. I will phone for help. If I see everything, I can tell the police everything. But I can't phone now. I can't move now, even to get my cell comm out to put it on silent. If my comm goes off, they'll know I'm here. There's a single spider's thread right next to my nose. It trembles too. The light from the crack makes it shine.

Through the darkness I strain to look at Anton, but I can't see what he's thinking and I pray *his* comm won't go off. And I look back through the crack in the ceiling.

19

Because I have to.

I have to know if it's Connor.

There, I've thought it. The unthinkable. I've been trying so hard not to. It could be Connor. I've known it could be Connor all along. He's weird. He put a live snail in the microwave once. I never told Mum. I should have, but we have this unspoken deal. He looks at me. His eyes say: You stay quiet. My eyes say: I'll stay quiet, but you don't hurt little Sally, because even though you're my brother – she's my sister too. Don't make me choose. He says: OK.

It can't be Connor. I don't want to believe it's Connor. I don't want it to be Connor. But deep down I know it could be. I don't trust him. Please God, don't let the tiles break.

They enter the library. They throw something into the library hallway. It explodes. It damages lockers. It stinks. They've got bombs!

If there's a fire, the Lock Down doors will open. I don't know if I'm hoping for a fire or not.

There are three of them now. No Connor. Thank God. I'm surprised. I hate myself for being surprised. I'm disappointed. I hate myself for being disappointed. I hate Connor. If he's not one of them, they may kill him. I'll be happy if they kill him; he's such a waste of space. But I must stop them, because I love Connor too. And I hate him. But he's just a stupid little moron in stupid trainers and he belongs to me. Nobody's allowed to kill him.

I know who they are now. They're suddenly easy to recognise. They're Lucas Bobb, Markel Mcleod and Jase. Damian's gang. Connor's in Damian's gang. They look around and Jase laughs like he knows there are over fifty Year Seven students, three teachers, a deputy head and a librarian hiding from him.

Nobody's ever hid from Jase before. Nobody's ever noticed Jase before. And the other two ain't special neither. Suddenly, with a shiver, I realise there's something wrong. It can't be just them. Jase? You gotta be kidding! Lucas Bobb, Markel Mcleod? Markel, maybe. But they couldn't have dreamed this up on their own. Someone's organised all this. How come they took so long to get from Theo and the humanities corridor to here? How come there are three of them now?

They've been somewhere, reported to someone, come here to carry on with some plan. This thing ain't random.

As Lucas enters, he shoots at a display case with Art Award book jackets in it. I did one of them. I did *Girl Meets Cake*. I did a big cake in the shape of a knight in shining armour and a girl rolling her eyes. I thought it was good. Splinters from the display case hit a kid who's hiding under a copier table near it.

Markel yells at everyone, 'We are the Eternal Knights. Get up!' His voice trails away like he ain't certain that anyone's going to do what he wants, even though he's got a gun.

When no one stands up, Markel says, 'I'll shoot anyway,' like there's an option. He fires at a desk. The shot bangs like a firework. He don't know some kid is under it. There's a whiff of gunsmoke. The kid is hit, but only in her arm.

Jase and Markel make their way down the side of the library, to two rows of computers. The kid hit in the arm uses the time to conceal herself behind the library counter. Another kid I recognise, called Rosie Perkins, is sitting curled up under a computer table. Jase drags her out, makes her lie on the floor.

The shooters set down their rucksacks. They open them. The bags are filled with ammunition. Full of ammunition! They reload their guns. They walk to the windows facing The Crossing. Jase says, 'There's someone getting away.' They both shoot through the windows at the staircase. I can't see who it is. I hope it's not Tariq. Glass shatters. It crashes. The light bounces off it. 'See if you can hit the Choco'n'Pop dispenser,' says Jase, like it's a game. He fires again. The library echoes like a shooting range.

Lucas joins them. They empty their weapons through the window into The Crossing, shooting at the Choco'n'Pop dispenser. Then they do some more reloading. I can't believe it. They've got about five guns each. Stuff like that costs money. Where the hell did they get all that money from? What's going on?

It's so quiet in the library. I've never heard it so quiet.

After a few seconds, Markel turns away from the broken windows overlooking the stairwell. He sees kids under a table. 'Come out,' he yells.

The kids don't move.

Markel is too lazy to bend down; he just fires his gun through the table. He hits the librarian. The rest, the kids hiding under it, spill out. There are three of them. Markel lines them up against the bookcases. He yells, 'If you gonna hide, we gonna execute you, like this.' He can't even say 'execute' properly; he says, 'extra-cute you' like it's a deal on hair shampoo or something. Then he puts a bullet through each of their foreheads. POW. POW. POW.

The kids drop. One of them is screaming. Then nothing.

Only the smell of gunshots, and the sound of windows rattling.

They just killed three kids. They're lying there like

dropped dolls. Nobody's saying nothing. The kids are just lying there. I can't believe it.

'See what we can do,' yells Markel.

Jase grabs his gun and walks over to the next row of computer desks. He's trying to be like Markel now. He fires his gun underneath the first desk in the row without even looking to see who's under it. The shot makes a lot of splinters but misses a kid who's hiding there. Jase shoots under the next computer desk. 'Come out,' he yells.

The Deputy Head, Miss Turnbull, is there. She's shot. She's hurt. Then Jase says, 'Damian says we're not gonna kill you if you stand up. Damian says we gotta make sure you come down to the gym. Damian says if you don't do as he says, we gonna have to kill you. All right?' He says this slowly, all American gangster, all clunky, like he's learned it by heart and is checking he got it right.

I look over at the corner where Ruby is hiding. Her feet are sticking out. I want to tell her to pull her feet in.

Lucas walks over to the table across from the lower computer row, slaps the top twice with his hand, kneels down, and says, 'Ready or not, here I come,' before dragging out a little Asian boy.

Lucas turns to the next table, where a student is squatted next to it rather than underneath it. She wasn't hidden enough. Three other little Year Sevens got there

24

first, so there wasn't enough room. Lucas asks her if she wants to die, or if she wants to go to the gym, and the girl says, 'Please don't kill me.' Lucas tells her to go and stand by the door. The kid gets up and goes over to stand by the door.

'See,' says Jase, like he's pleased he got that right. 'Damian says you gotta line up.'

I can see straight away that Jase is a moron who's just following orders. He is so moronic that obviously if Damian said, 'Shoot everyone in the bollocks,' he'd even try to do that to the girls. It's not funny. Damian's not funny. I don't know him and I don't want to. My friend Adrianna knew him. She said she was in his bedroom once, and all the walls were covered with pictures of guns: guns on their own, guns held by gangsters, guns from the past, guns in holsters, shotguns, revolvers, BB guns, Macs, just guns and guns and guns. When she dumped him he stalked her down the street and across the Internet, and sent her pictures of the guns he was going to use to kill her, until her family, in desperation, relocated back to Krakow or somewhere. Clever Adrianna.

I try to remember if Connor ever said anything about Damian. But Connor don't say much other than he'll show us all one day. He actually ain't spoken to no one in the family for months. If he wants something he just points and grunts. You can get a lot across by grunting. He gets it across to us very clearly. He says: I don't want none of you to ask me nuffing, and Mum should hand over all her money.

Even if you want to ask Connor about something, there's never a right time. If he ain't asleep, he's just going to sleep. If he's alone, he's playing the box and right at a tricky you-must-not-disturb-me point. If he's finished playing the box, he's in a temper because he lost, or he's too excited because he won. Believe me there's never a right time.

Lucas starts to walk over towards the quiet corner. My heart stops. Little Ruby's legs are still sticking out. But before Lucas can get there, Markel moves to back up Jase and drags Miss Turnbull out from under the desk. 'Tell them to line up or we're gonna have to shoot them all,' he says. Like he's already tired of shooting people, and it's all become too much like hard work. He says it with this kind of be-sorry-for-me whine in his voice.

Lucas stops. He's noticed the whine in Markel's voice. He listens to what's happening between Markel and the Deputy Head. He don't quite reach the pile of beanbags. He just ducks his head round the corner of the quiet place, fires a couple of shots at random into the bags without properly looking. He fires at the books and the low tables and turns back. He rolls his eyes at an imaginary camera. He even kisses his teeth, copying Markel. Like killing people is such a boring thing. He keeps looking at Markel, ready to copy him to the max. And I wonder why. In an instant I figure it out. Lucas is scared. He's scared of something. Not Markel though. Markel is the answer. I can tell Lucas thinks that if he does everything Markel does, and feels just the way Markel feels, then he's safe.

Lucas shrugs, like he's done with the quiet corner. He turns away. Thank God. Please let him turn away. I hold my breath. He's walking back towards the computer hub. He's more interested in what Markel is going to do to Miss Turnbull. I catch my heart as I search the beanbags for blood. Please let Ruby be OK.

Lucas is back at the computer hub. He does a little jump, like he's dead excited to see poor Miss Turnbull clutching at her side and dragging herself off the floor. Markel is waving the gun everywhere.

'Tell them,' Markel insists, but Miss Turnbull don't say nothing.

And it's funny that even though Markel's got a gun, and he's got two morons who're trying to do exactly what he does, he still needs Miss Turnbull to tell the Year Sevens what to do.

Markel tries to pull Miss Turnbull to her feet, but he

can't. He calls to Jase and Lucas to help him. All three of them stand there not knowing what to do with her. She won't stand up and she won't say nothing. Markel kneels down and pushes the gun in her face. 'Tell them to line up!' he yells so hard I can see spit spewing out of his mouth.

'He's got a gun,' says Jase, stating the obvious, like that will somehow convince her to do what they want.

She's breathing hard. She says, 'Do you promise no one will be hurt, if I tell them to line up?'

Markel just yells, 'Do as I say or I swear I'll kill everyone.'

Wearily Miss Turnbull crawls to her feet. 'Do what they say,' she calls into the silent library.

There's a shuffling and a rustling and a peeping out from hiding places. Miss Turnbull drags herself up and is leaning on the desks, making her way to the door. The maths teacher for Year Seven follows her, crawling out from under the printer table. Then another two teachers appear and a few students as well.

'Go on! Go on!' urges Jase.

Gradually the little Year Sevens twist themselves out of desks and shelves and cupboards and follow Miss Turnbull. One after the other they form a ragged line by the door. I look down at the pile of beanbags. Ruby's face is peeping out. There's blood on it. I don't think she can move. But she's alive. At least she's alive.

Very slowly I inch back the ceiling tile. When there's enough space I'm going to stick my head out. I'm going to let Ruby know what's going on. It's a gamble. One hell of a gamble. But they won't look up unless I make a noise, and I don't think Lucas will be back to the quiet corner, not yet. And Markel's too caught up with making sure Miss Turnbull does what he says. And Jase is using every last brain cell, which is more than he started with, to make sure the kids are lining up.

So I lean down out of the ceiling until I am sure Ruby can see me. She looks up. I motion her to stay put. I mouth: They. Are. Going. I give her the thumbs-up. I pat the air, telling her to wait.

Ruby rests her head on the floor and closes her eyes. I want to scream at her, 'Don't die. Don't you dare die. Not now!'

Her eyes half flutter open like she can hear me.

She looks up again.

I can't bear the look in her eyes.

They're asking for something she knows I can't give.

But I can. I will give it. Somehow.

I will help you, Ruby.

# 9.57 a.m.
## Friday, 18 September

For a split second we hold our gaze, then very slowly Ruby opens her mouth. She mouths something at me. She's trying to tell me something. I freeze. Maybe she can see something from the book corner I've missed. I daren't turn my head. I don't trust myself to get my head back inside the ceiling. I won't be able to reset the tile. I'm trembling. I can't help it. I can't stop it. Just stay very still, I tell myself. The library's gone drop-dead silent. If you move now, you stupid moron, you're going to end up dead. I'm stuck with my head poking out the ceiling. I stare down at Ruby, trying to understand what she means. Then I know. Markel is doing a last check round. He's heading my way. Thank God I *didn't* move. Pray God he don't look up.

I want to close my eyes but it's like they're stuck open. Markel is passing right under me, right now. Don't look up. I daren't even blink. Lucas and Jase are trying to line up the students. But they never lined up in their lives, let alone lined nobody else up, so they don't know how to do it. Markel's going back. Thank God. Jase is repeating and repeating, 'Line. Up. Line. Up,' and waving his gun like if he shoots them, they're going to line up straighter. Lucas don't care. He's busy smashing up a computer like that's the funnest thing.

Markel is heading back their way. I still can't move. He wanders around threatening to put a bullet through anyone left alive who ain't lining up. My heart is pounding so hard I feel dizzy. But mostly the kids are helping the wounded to stand up, and that's part of the line-up problem. Like how can you do single file when you've got to lean on someone? My arms are aching now with holding my position. I can't flex or nothing. Markel hurries; poking about under the tables like the library is already haunted. He don't go into the quiet corner. Thank God. Instead he picks up a fallen backpack, rifles through it and nicks a cell comm. Then he poses to his own reflection in a bookcase window making I Am De Badman faces.

'Oi,' he yells at last. 'Move.'

The line straggles out through the swing door and turns towards the gym.

I pull my head back in. At last. I lie there shaking and shaking. I can't move even to get out my cell. After what seems like an age, I roll over on my back and pull it out of my pocket. My beat-up, broken, bottom-of-the-range cell communicator with its bust casing. I turn it on. In the blue light it casts, I can see Anton lying there.

'What d'you do that for?' he hisses.

I look at him blank.

'You could've got us killed.'

I don't say nothing. Nothing about Ruby and how he pushed her out, and how she's hit and how I feel. Nothing about the three little kids.

'They gone?' he whispers.

I still don't answer. I don't understand. I simply lie there. But I do understand. I've seen this before in the classroom but nobody got killed. But I've seen this madness, this I-don't-give-a-shit, this Who-cares-you-can't-do-nothing-to-me, so-try-and-stop-me, and then I-think-I-will-just-destroy-whatever-I-can. I was in one class when a boy set fire to the desk at the back. It caught up pretty quick and burned down all the computer hubs near it. He was laughing as we tried to get out. He thought seeing us falling over ourselves trying to survive was the most exciting thing he'd ever seen.

When they hauled him up to the Head's office, she gave him fairy cakes and asked him to tell her all about his problems.

'Did you see them go?' Anton says again. He reaches

32

out to me in this luminous darkness where you can't see a bleeding thing. Somehow my eyes adjust. Somehow light seeps through. He grabs my hand. His hand is warm. '*Have they gone?*'

I think I saw them go, but I'm so scared. I don't know any more. Maybe they're still down there. I don't know anything, except I want him to be quiet. 'Shush,' I say and he shushes.

I put my cell comm on silent. I call the police. But I'm too scared to make a noise so I let it ring. I hear the woman pick up and say, 'Fire, ambulance, police,' and other stuff. But I daren't answer. I try to whisper, 'Police,' but it won't come out. I'm scared. I hang up. Then I think, *Get down and see if anyone's alive. Help them first. Help Ruby.* Then I think, *Text the police.* But you can't text the police. So I think text someone then, but not Mum. Mum won't be no use. But I don't want anyone to call me. I'd have to speak. And I don't want my comm to lose battery. My comm is very old and the battery can run down just for anything.

But I got to text someone. Someone who'll help. And I remember Gilly at Latchkey Club and I know she'll be sensible, so I text her.

I write: **Gilly plse call t police der r sum boys in r school wit guns n they just killed kids n t library. Not a joke**

33

n please don't call me bcos hiding from them. Leah. I send it.

Within seconds I get a text back. I can feel the soft vibration of the cell comm slipping in my hand. It feels huge, like an earthquake. I open her message up. **I'll call the police. If this a joke you are SO going to be in serious trouble. Gilly.**

I pass the phone to Anton. He reads it and his face is blank. Greeny-yellowy blank in the half-light.

And I know what I got to do. And I got to do it, because I'm not a loser like Aliesha. I'm in control, ain't I? But it's still hard. That's what you don't understand. You see me like this, and you think being me and being in control is easy, and It's. All. Right. For. Leah. But it ain't like that. I'm just as scared the hell out, as you all are. But I got to put all that to one side. I got to make the hardest decision ever in my life. I got to decide to get down out the ceiling. I'm not thinking straight. I got to help Ruby. I promised I would. Hell no, I should just stay here. I got to check to see if anyone else is alive. They might be covered in blood, but however much covered in blood, I got to help. I am so not thinking straight. Hide them, up here or somewhere? Those killers might come back. They might do anything. I'm the only person who can help right now, unless Anton will.

And I know before even asking, Anton won't.

He won't help. He's too smart. He knows that risking himself to help someone who might die anyway is not all that clever. And Anton is clever. That's why I like him. He may go to YOU OP 78 but that don't mean nothing. Except that YOU OP 78 is a dump school for kids whose parents are on Extreme Hardship Benefits. At least it don't mean you ain't smart. It means you won't get an education that'll take you anywhere much, and it means your folks can't get any lower in the pecking order, but it don't mean you ain't smart.

'Leah?'

I look at him. He knows what I'm thinking. He knows me, like he knows all those books he reads. He won't answer me, though. He won't move. I think he'll move if he knows the killers ain't coming back, though. He looks like he wet himself and is hoping his pee ain't soaked through the ceiling tiles and given him away. And I don't blame him, because I know I look like that too.

I don't know what to do. My heart is banging and tumbling around from my throat to my legs. I think I might throw up. I'm slippy with sweat, but it's like a cold sweat. I think I must be in shock. I peer through the crack again. I can see Ruby. She's got her eyes closed. I have a choice: I can lie here and hope the police get through and save me and save them and stop those shooters, or I can do something myself, and maybe help someone and maybe save a life.

And maybe lose mine.

And I know what I want to do, but I know what I *ought* to do. If it was Sally down there. If I was down there what I'd want me to do. But it's not me down there. I'm up here and I'm safe. Not very safe, but safer. All I got to do is stay still and wait. The police will come. I peer out of the ceiling again, trying to decide. Help is going to come. The police are going to come any minute. They're going to storm this building and then I'll get down.

Ruby's hand moves. She moans.

I can't stay here and listen to her dying. I just can't. I wish I could. I try to. I pull my head back in. I really, really try hard. I shove my fingers in my ears and stay still. After all, I called the police; that's helping, ain't it? They're supposed to take over now. But I can't. I'm lifting off the upside-down tile and placing it gently beside me. I'm peering out. I'm looking at her twitching hand. Her eyelids flutter again. Her eyes meet mine. There's a language eyes have. I never knew that. Her eyes are talking. They're saying, '*Please help me. I'm hurt bad. I'm*

36

bleeding. *I'm scared. Please help me. I'll do anything, if only you'll help me.*'

And I remember I promised myself I'd help her somehow.

I'm slipping my legs through the ceiling space. I'm judging the size of the drop. I'm going to have to twist to make it on to the librarian's counter. But I can make it. It ain't no more than five metres and if I lower myself to my fingertips, I'll make it.

I turn to Anton. 'I'm going down,' I say.

'You're crazy,' he says.

'Probably,' I say.

'There's no future in being crazy,' he says. 'Wait for the police.'

'I don't care,' I say. 'Sometimes you got to do something to change the future.'

He smiles like I'm a sad moron.

'And that time just arrived,' I say.

And then I swing out of the ceiling and twist and get ready to let drop.

# 10.20 a.m.
## Friday, 18 September

I lower my legs down through the hole. I try to position the tile so it will flop back into place. Already I've worked out that I can't drag tables on to tables and top them up with chairs now. If one of the Eternals hears, they'll come back. I'm only safe if they think everyone in the library is dead.

My mind is working overtime: how will I get back up into the ceilings? That's the safest place. I know it is. Anton's right. He's always right. I turn my head and look at the drop down, and decide I can climb up on one of the bookshelves against the wall and move a tile out there and get back in.

I drop. The tile gently plops back behind me. I land as softly as a cat. I never knew I could land like that. My toes curl into the counter surface and immediately I crouch down. It's not just noise. It's movement, too, that can give me away. I slip from the counter to the floor. I look around. I can't believe it. They've really gone.

Quickly I race to Ruby. She's trembling. She's bleeding, but her eyes are thanking me. She's been shot through the hand, other places too. The bones in her fingers must have deflected the bullet. It passed through; maybe it's in her chest. I hope not. It's bleeding a lot. It's only flesh, ain't it?

I whisper in her ear. 'It'll be all right.'

Her eyes thank me. And I can't bear it. I got to look away. There is no way I can get her into the ceiling. The shooters might come back. I can't leave her just lying here, neither. I try not to think about the others. The ones left behind lying out of sight – over by the computers. If they're alive, they're lying very still. You can't be alive if you are shot in the head, can you? I can't help anyone if they're not alive. I look down at my thin arms. I can't lift anyone into the ceilings, neither.

The book cupboard. I remember. I can put Ruby in the book cupboard. I was the library monitor for two terms. I helped Miss do the displays. I helped Miss run the Meridian Book Awards. I put boxes of books in the book cupboard.

Miss is dead.

The keys to the book cupboard will be round her neck on her teacher name tag. I crawl over to the library counter and from there to the table. From far away comes a rally of shots. They're somewhere else shooting. Shooting someone else.

Where's Connor? I don't have to think about Connor right now.

Miss Fish was pretty. She was young and pretty.

Where the hell are the police?

Miss Fish is lying in a pool of blackening blood. Her fingers are curled up around the corner of a book. The back of her head is gone. I don't want to look at it. I got to get the keys off her. I got to lift up her head and un-loop the tag around her neck. I got to.

Her head slips under my touch. 'I'm sorry,' I breathe, as if she's still alive. I'm so sorry. My face is shaking, and my eyes are filling up, and her head is so slippy to hang on to. I don't want to touch it. I stuff my hand down under her and root around until I feel the hard edge of her name tag. I slide my fingers round it and find the keys; then very carefully I drag my hand out and loop the key chain off her neck over the mess that was her head.

I never knew I could do this. I can't do this, but my hands and fingers and legs and knees are doing it. I'm crawling across the floor back to Ruby.

'It'll be all right,' I say again, like the record is stuck in my head, like we're in some kind of time warp, or on a trip to the dentist. Nothing is OK. Nothing will be all right. I've just seen the inside of Miss Fish's skull and her brains in blobbish gluey lumps and I've touched them, and there are kids with guns loose in the school and they'll kill me.

The school messaging intercom suddenly crackles into life. Somebody giggles at mega decibels into the system. Somebody whispers in a fake horror voice, 'You wanna die, punk?' and giggles again. But this is not a fake horror show; this is real and I don't want to die.

I pull Ruby up. I drag her. She's much heavier than she looks. I heave her to the book cupboard. 'I'm so thirsty,' she whispers.

I say, 'It'll be all right.' I punch in the door coordinates and unlock the book cupboard. The door creaks open, making a terrifying noise. I switch the light on. It's a long, narrow kind of cupboard with stacks of shelves lining one wall. I drag Ruby in as far as I can. There's plenty of room. I need to switch off the light. But I can't leave her in the dark, can I? But I am going to leave her. I'm going to get back up in the ceilings, where it's safer, and where I can move slowly out towards the exits. To the exits through the mess of wiring and pipes. As soon as Lock Down finishes, I'm out of here. Then I can get help for Ruby. That's what I tell myself. But that's not why. I just want to get out. I want to be near clever

Anton. I want to save my own miserable skin. The police must come soon.

Inside the book cupboard, I prop Ruby up. I fetch her a beanbag. I tell her, 'I'm going for help. I'll lock you in. If they come back you'll be safe. Don't make a noise.'

Her eyes tell me that she's saying, '*Yes, please hurry, please don't leave me, please get help, please don't go, please don't let them get me*.' Like I can control them.

I say, 'It'll be all right.' And I leave her and lock the door behind her. That's when I notice the blood smears on the floor and the drag marks, and anyone can see that someone dragged themselves into the book cupboard. Plus there's a light shining out from under it. So I unlock the door again and put off the light. Ruby whimpers. 'I'm scared of the dark,' she says.

'Don't be scared,' I say. 'The dark won't shoot you, but if those boys see the light, they will.'

'OK,' she whispers.

'Can I get something else?' I say, like I can replace light with anything.

'Choco,' she says.

'OK,' I say. I don't know why I say that. I just want to get out.

Then I take off my jacket and rub the floor with it until all traces of Ruby, locked and bleeding and thirsty

42

# 10.50 a.m.
## Friday, 18 September

And I lie there, staring up into the darkness in that ceiling. Wondering. And I can't believe I just did what I just did. I just got down and got keys off a dead teacher and locked a wounded student in a book cupboard and if you'd asked me this morning if that was something I could ever do, I'd look at you like you was gone mental.

And the darkness all around me is throbbing and bulging and pressing down on me. I'm lying here like it's a real weight, and I'm thinking: *What The Hell Am I Going To Do? What The Hell?* And I can still smell blood. It's on my hands. It stinks. And there's this weird thing going on with my teeth. It feels like they've grown huge in my face and they're so big I can't close my mouth. And I'm trying to believe what's happened, but trying to believe it is making me go crazy. This can't be happening. This don't happen. The government has stopped all this kind of stuff. The police will come. Since the second lot of riots,

45

when they burned down the schools, burned down the town halls, burned enough police stations, they cut the benefits to everyone not in Extreme Hardship With Kids and did away with senseless violence. They did. I know they did. I saw it on telly. That's what they said. They said it. They did it. They was robust and everything and busted crime. My teeth feel so huge I put my hand up to my mouth. I realise I'm clenching my teeth together so tight my jaw is locked.

I rub gently at the sides of my face, trying to get my teeth to relax. A single spider's thread is dangling out of the darkness, trembling, shuddering with my breath. There must be enough spiders up here. What am I going to do? I don't care about spiders. They don't have guns. I can't leave Ruby locked up in a cupboard.

I got to do something. I got to submit my Five Minutes of Fame and Fortune files. Too late now. It's a really Big Deal as well. If I do good, I get a scholarship. Why am I thinking about that? Like it even matters. But it matters to me. Where are the police? Did Gilly really call them? Call them again. I got to get out. I got to find Connor. But wait, if he is one of them and the police come – maybe they'll kill him. Maybe I shouldn't call them again? Where *is* Connor?

\* \* \*

46

Connor.

He comes out the bathroom. He looks like he thinks it's his birthday. Best T-shirt, best camouflage jeans, best trainers; the ones he keeps in the box on the shelf over his bed with the price tag still on them, so that every idiot friend of his who goes in there can see he's a moron like them, and ready to waste ninety pounds on a pair of trainers that were designed for Olympic athletes and are owned by a fat kid who never leaves the sofa, and even if he did, can't really put them on, because they don't really fit.

Moron.

Connor.

Ninety pounds. Do you know what ninety pounds can buy? It can fill a supermarket trolley. A proper big deep trolley. It can pay three months of heating bills. It could pay for eighteen trips to parks and museums and adventure playgrounds for Sally with a sandwich and an ice cream each time if we shared.

All that wasted.

Connor.

He can hardly walk in them anyway. He got a size too small, because they're cheaper in kids' sizes.

That's how desperate he is to be a moron.

I say, 'It's only Own Clothes Day.' I'm trying to be sarcastic. Like is this what it's all about? Why not bully money out of your depressed mother and dump out on your little sister and

47

*piss off your bigger sister, who is practically the only one who cares for you, and spoil her chances, just so you can look stupid and hobble around in front of morons. But my point is lost. And anyway 'it's only Own Clothes Day' for students who can pay a pound for Children in Need to their tutors, which Connor can't.*

*Although he'd probably qualify.*

*For Children in Need.*

*Or euthanasia.*

*Connor.*

*Connor don't answer. He's like that. Mum calls it The Silent Stage if she calls it anything, if she's OK long enough to even notice that Connor ain't speaking again.*

*Connor.*

*Moron.*


I'm shaking. I shouldn't have called the police. *What if Connor is one of them?* It's too late. I must find him. Of course I should've called the police. Forget Connor. If he is one of them he deserves to get shot. Ruby's hurt. They've got all the kids. I got to do my Five Minutes of Fame and Fortune. I got to get out. The police will come. They have to come.

But a thought seems to come back at me from the darkness. *You can't get out. Everywhere's Locked Down. You'll never get out. Everyone will die and they'll kill Connor. You'll be too late to get your Five Minutes filed and you won't go to college.*

Anton is right. There's no future. Suddenly I'm sobbing. My body is contracting and shaking in great, huge, soundless sobs. Tears are rolling down my cheeks and I can't stop – until I realise they might soak through the ceiling and give me away. Then I stop straight, just like that. And I'm crying, but no tears are coming out and that's that.

When at last my jaw can move a little bit, I open it and whisper into the darkness. 'Anton?'

I hear a slight intake of breath, like he's so shitting himself, he's too scared to speak. He probably heard me crying.

I whisper louder, 'Anton?'

And I hear a slight, 'Yeah?'

I hear him ask, 'She going to be OK?'

I don't know. Maybe she is, maybe she's not. I just don't know. So I say, 'Maybe.'

'Good,' he says, like that means yes.

'What're we gonna do?' I say.

But he ain't got no answers, so I lie there. I'm not interested any more in sobbing, or trying to loosen up my jaw, or get my mind to start working, because it is working, and I'm thinking, what am I going to do? I got to stay alive. I'm going to stay alive. College don't matter if you're dead. I got to help Ruby. The police will come. And I got to help Connor if I can. I got to get us all out.

So I lie there and lie there and think what to do first. I go over and over it. Round and round it repeats in my brain. I feel my cell comm buzz in my pocket. First of all find a safe place to call out and let them know about Ruby – she needs a doctor badly. I got to let Connor know about the police. He never checks his texts. *I need to tell Connor*. I could call him maybe. Then I could check the exits. Then we got to wait for the police and that's it.

I roll over, gently, in the darkness, gingerly on to my side. I hiss out at Anton, 'I'm going down.'

'What?' he says. I can hear the shock in his voice.

'Got to,' I say.

'Why?'

'Connor might be one of them. I got to call him. I got to find him; let him know about the police coming; get him out.'

'You think he's in with them?'

'Dunno.'

'Why would you think that?'

I bite my lip. Where should I start? There's no easy place. It's like asking when did you start hiding the kitchen knives? It wasn't when Connor was eight and

50

slipped a steak knife into his sock and went out to reclaim the park, was it? He was just tiny then, short for his age and only 'arming' himself because 'others' did. It wasn't when I found the vegetable peeler gone. That short sharp little stabber: just not there. I had to try and fix potatoes with the bread knife that evening. I made a joke: 'crinkle-cut spuds'. No, I just woke up one morning and decided I'd better hide the knives. I never asked why or why now? I just hid them and felt a lot better.

'I dunno,' I say.

'Then why?'

I don't answer.

'Aren't you interested in why?'

'Nope,' I say. I'm not interested in WHY.

'I mean the BIG WHY?'

'Like why do kids go on the rampage and kill each other? That kind of why?'

'Yeah,' says Anton.

That's him all over. He don't like to deal with here and now. He likes to put all that in a box called Later. Then he fast forwards to Later and examines it like it was a computer that he could hack into and make it give up all its secrets. He likes hacking into computers. But you can't really hack into reality, can you?

And anyway we all know the reasons.

1 Bad parenting. (So, bit late to put that right, ain't it?)

2 Peer pressure. (Which one of them is the peer? I remember an art teacher telling my mum: 'Connor is all right. He's just about as good as the kid he sits next to.' 'Cept Connor always chose to sit next to the bad kids until their mums complained about him being a bad influence.)

3 Poverty. (If that was the case by now all of Africa should have shot itself stupid long since.)

4 Low self-esteem. (Yeah, well, you don't get given respect, do you? You got to earn it by doing something respectable.)

5 Society. (Nice one.)


Yeah, you can always shift the blame someplace else. Maybe that's the real problem. Nobody being willing to own up. All of them claiming to be the victim whilst victimising everyone else.

Anyway, I think kids do it because they like to. It's fun. Jase sure liked trying to get those kids to line up. Lucas was having the time of his life following Markel around. But that's another problem. Why would you *like* doing stuff like that? So that your 'peers' get 'nuff respect'? So you can settle old scores? 'Yo, go on. Show them. Blow their brains out. Then they'll know.'

Then they do it cos they can. I guess. Maybe because their big sister never tried to figure out why she hid the knives. It's all suddenly too much. I'm shaking again. 'No, Anton,' I repeat. 'I'm not interested in WHY.'

'But in the future,' he says, 'historians will ask: why here, why now, why them?'

'That's their shit,' I whisper. 'Are you going to help me or what?'

'OK,' he says. And for some reason I'm surprised. I kind of thought he might lie up here in the ceilings pondering the causes and the consequences and whether in the great scheme of things today was going to change history or not.

'This had to happen,' he says.

'I don't see why,' I say.

'Have you ever wondered what exactly the role of YOU OP Academies is?' he says.

Anton sure asks some stupid questions.

'If they're for limiting social mobility and keeping the underclass down, why is that better than a proper education, producing workers that have a higher net worth, that improve the economy?'

'Anton?' I say. And I know he *is* pondering like I thought.

'So they should have seen it coming,' he continues. 'When you undereducate an entire generation, when you have kids who know all their rights and take none of their responsibilities, when you know they need to belong to something – but they don't feel like they belong to nothing, when they parent kids and are only kids themselves . . .'

If this is his idea of helping, I'm sorry I asked.

'When society is happy to see them fighting each other and doesn't step in to change anything, when they feel belittled in a system that has already discarded them, when they are disillusioned, humiliated, vengeful, when they see no future for themselves, when they decide to take power into their own hands . . .'

'When you shut up,' I say, 'we can do something.'

'OK,' he says again. And I want to hug him, because he shoves everything up into his brain and tries to find reasons and answers and all and spout it out like he's going to write it in a book, but right now the only thing that's going to help us is getting out.

'We've got to *do* something,' I say. 'Where're the police?'

He don't say nothing. It's like he's debating the relative benefits of action versus non-action, and non-action is winning.

'If we try and slither around too much in these ceilings we're going to break some tiles and give ourselves away,' I say. 'There are other ceilings in other rooms; there must be acres of ceilings we can hide in.'

And Anton still don't say nothing. I can hear him breathing – huge, sickening, shuddering breaths.

'The police should be here by now,' I whisper. 'I'm gonna send Gilly another text.'

I text Gilly a second time: **It's me, Gilly, the police didn't come yet. Plse call again – there's kids who've been shot. It's bad. Plse get us out.**

I even try to call the police myself. I dial. I whisper, 'There's shooters in YOU OP 78. Please help us.' But the voice on the other end says, 'This is an automated service. Since the Bill of 2018 all police lines employ automated services. Your call will be recorded. What you say may be used in evidence. Please speak clearly. Do you want fire, ambulance or police?'

'Police,' I whisper. I daren't speak any louder.

'I'm sorry, I didn't quite get that. Please speak loudly and clearly into the handset,' says the automated voice.

It's no use. I hang up. 'We got to do something,' I hiss at Anton.

But Anton's staring at me and breathing in that horrible way. And he don't reply, which is somehow annoying.

I don't know what I'm expecting, maybe a plan, a suggestion, something we can do about Ruby. But Anton stays quiet and don't say a thing. Maybe he don't want to do anything.

'I'm going to go then,' I say. 'There's got to be a way out.'

'You're crazy,' he says at last. There's something in his tone. He's figured something out. 'Survival is all that counts, Leah. Stay here. Stay put. Wait it out.'

My heart sinks. So he ain't going to help after all.

'But what about Ruby then?' I say, which is a mean thing to say, because I know he must be feeling pretty bad about her, but maybe she ain't got enough time to wait it out.

'It's a less risky choice,' he says.

Very carefully I edge forward on the tiles. Wriggling along on tiles is not easy. Not when they're made of the thinnest, cheapest polystyrene and can crack into a zillion little white pieces at the slightest twitch. But I'm careful. I feel for each strut, each joist. My hands are shaking, my heart's pumping like it could spill blood out and replace all the blood that's been spilled all over.

'Maybe there's a way out.'

I carry on wriggling.

'Anton?' I hiss. But he don't say nothing. 'I'm going to

see if I can do something,' I say again, not sure why the frick I keep saying it – why I'm not staying put like him and holing up and lying there. It can't go on long. I should stay put. The police will come. They have to. The army will come. The government will do something. Nobody's just going to leave us here. But my hands aren't thinking like me, because they're still lifting a tile back and peering out, checking.

Down there in the library everything's eerily quiet. No moans, no more screams, only the ticking of the standard-issue clock.

'Lee,' says Anton unexpectedly.

I swivel round to look at him.

'If you don't make it,' he says, his voice squeaking a little, 'I want you to know.'

I nod.

'I'm going to stay up here.'

I nod.

'You understand, don't you?'

'Yeah,' I say.

'I got to survive,' he says. 'I got to survive and I got to do it my way. That's the deal.'

'Yeah,' I say.

'You have the same choice.'

'Yeah,' I say.

'But I'll try and help. I'll try and use my comm to see if I can hack into the security system and release Lock Down. I'll jingle you if I can. My sig tune – over the PA system.' He laughs. 'Then you'll know. I'll try to intercept any calls being made and let you know what's happening too. I'll get someone new to call the police. That's all I can do.'

I smile. 'Please don't do anything too easy,' I say. Hacking into Lock Down must be like trying to access CIA files from the Pentagon.

'I'll do what I think best. That's the deal.'

I nod.

'I just wanted you to know.'

I nod again. There's so much to say. We don't say none of it. I slide the tile back into place. There must be a way out. There must be safer places, boiler rooms with safety doors and places where you can keep injured kids and not be found, where the sound of water cisterns and heating systems will hide the sound of you calling out, will hide the sound of moaning.

I haul myself across the tiles. I think about whispering 'Bye' and 'I want you to know something too' and 'If we ever get out . . .'. I want to say, 'Yeah, I get the deal, you've got to look after Number One, but what if your brother was out there, and you didn't do something to

58

save him? And he died. What if you didn't even try, and you found out later you could have? What would you tell yourself afterwards?' But what's the point? I don't blame him. I want to survive too. I peer through the semi-gloom. Everybody got to do what they got to do. That's the deal.

I get to the edge of some kind of wall that's been built up through the ceiling, supporting it, I guess. Looks easy enough to get over, but what's on the other side? In the darkness, I've lost direction. My comm buzzes. It's been buzzing a bit. I daren't get it out right now. That'd mean rolling sideways and the last time I did that a tile cracked. If I could stay up here in the ceiling and inch on until I find a way out, I'd be OK, but I'm not sure I'm even going the right way. Plus I got to try and contact Connor. I got to get to a place where my voice won't give me away. All the exits are going to be on ground level. All the secure storage and boiler rooms are going to be on the lower-ground level. There's no way I can go downstairs like this.

I got to get down then. Get out of the ceiling. The idea of getting down on to the corridors scares the hell out of me, like parachuting into enemy territory. I lever the front of my body up on the wall. The decking of Level A above me is much higher up than I thought. My eyes are getting used to the gloom too. Where the striplights are below, the tiles glow with an eerie light. You get used to it, and it's enough to see by. You'd think the place would be full of dust, but it ain't. It's like it's been all sealed up till we broke in, like a pharaoh's tomb. I straddle my feet on either side of a tile joist and then I squat there, shaking. I stretch upward. I could probably stand up. I can't stay here, can I? I mean, I could stay here, but then what if Aliesha is bleeding to death in Lab One and I didn't try and help her? If I was bleeding out in Lab One I'd want someone to try and help me.

I force the image of Aliesha bleeding out in Lab One away. Find a way to get out. Save yourself. When you're out you can tell someone about Aliesha. That's the best way to help her. You're not a bleeding surgeon, are you?

I prise back the tile in front of me. It snaps out of its setting with a slight pop. I tense up ready for a bullet. But nothing happens. After an age of squatting there and tensing, eventually I peer down. I'm over B corridor. There's a wall display board just a little to my left. Posters of Volunteer Programmes flap on it, all jazzed up in shiny 3D images. What a rip off. Volunteer Programmes, that's just a fancy name for No More Education.

I check the corridor below. I wait. At last a chance to check my phone. I pull it out. There's a list of messages but none from the police, none from Connor, none from

Mum. I push it back in my pocket. They're not important. I'll read them later. I need to find somewhere I can call out properly.

I got to be really sure no one's about. I eye the Volunteer Programme posters again. They tell me once I leave YOU OP Academy and go to a Volunteer Programme I'll be doing a real job and that's like such a big deal. They tell me it's For the Greater Good and it'll get me ready for my role in the Big Society. They tell me, in shiny, silver-edged 3D writing, I'll get allowances: a daily bus card and one canteen voucher every day. They don't tell me my education'll be finished.

I clamber out of the ceiling and jump myself down into B corridor.

Immediately I know it's a big mistake.

A HUGE one.

All corridors have CCTV.

And B corridor is no exception.

Somewhere those kids are watching. Somewhere they've hooked themselves up to the CCTV. I know this for certain because a voice bellows out over the public address system.

'LEAH JACKSON ON LEVEL ONE, B CORRIDOR. GIVE YOURSELF UP. LIE ON THE FLOOR, YOU WASTER. WE'RE COMING TO GET YOU.'

61

# 11.10 a.m.
## Friday, 18 September

Holy shit. How stupid.

Stupid. Stupid. Stupid.

I scan the corridor. Nobody. They're going to send someone, aren't they? More Jase and Markel? Well, I ain't laying in no dirty corridor waiting to get shot in the back of the head. I sprint to the CCTV camera. Before I disappear, I want to check one thing. I stretch up on tiptoe. The angle of the camera can't see the ceilings or right close to the walls. It's like I thought, but I needed to check. I heave a breath out. Nobody saw me coming out of the ceiling. If they run the tape back, which they won't, they'll think I stepped out of a classroom. I don't stop to check nothing else. I give them the finger. I turn. I run.

Down B corridor counting the CCTV cameras, one at each corner, one by the lockers. They've got fricking cameras everywhere. Nowhere to hide. Know where to hide? My breath is bursting out, like my chest is a bleeding hairdryer. I'm sweating. I get to the end of B corridor. I got to hide. I got to get back in the ceilings. I've locked Ruby in a bleeding book cupboard. If I die, she'll die all locked up in the darkness. I'm not going to fricking die. Why the frick did I get down on to a corridor? I should have known. Run. Think. Run faster. Think where the hell you're going. Where don't they have CCTV?

In the classroom.

They don't have CCTV in the classrooms.

Which classroom? How can I fool them? I'm running. I'm thinking and I'm thinking, get back into the science labs, because they all link together through the tech dens – and if you get into the first one, they won't know which one you disappeared from. They were there. There'll be a mess. Maybe somehow in the mess they'll miss you.

So I turn and sprint for the stairwell. I make it. The address system is yelling at me. 'LEAH JACKSON. WE'LL GET YOU. YOU'RE GOING TO DIE.'

I figure it. They haven't started out yet. They're watching, waiting for me to run myself into a hole then they'll track me down. My breathing eases a little. I try to think, whose voice is that? The more I know, the more I can tell the police. Because they ain't going to get me. But the police need to get here quickly. When I get to a safe place I'll call out; I will get to one. I know I will. I have to.

63

'YOU'RE GOING TO DIE, LEAH JACKSON.' The voice ends in a stupid snigger. A wave of anger flares in my cheeks. I feel it burning. Being chased by a moron like Jase, by Markel? Do they think I'm mad? Do they think they can kill me and I'll do nothing to stop them? Up ahead is a door. I sprint. Do they think I'm going to lie down and wait for their stupid bullets? My life ain't theirs. I swing into the first lab and check to make sure there's no CCTV. They're taking the piss.

No CCTV. Thank Sweet Jesus. But I don't stop. I sprint back through biology 1 and biology 2, through the tech dens with their jars of evil stuff lining the walls, frogs floating in formaldehyde, all bloated and pale, snakes pinned open, other things: pigs' lungs or goats or something. The PA system starts again. 'LEAH JACKSON, YOU'RE A STUPID BITCH. COME OUT OF—'

Suddenly the sound cuts. There's a silence, then a little jingle. It's Frank Sinatra with 'I Did It My Way', Anton's jingle. Anton just hacked into the PA system and shut it down. Thank you, Anton. God bless you, Anton. You did help even if you were looking after Number One. I look at the benches and the shelves and the cupboards. When I decide which one, I'll stop and climb up on that stuff and pick out a tile and get myself into the ceiling again. If I'm careful I can disappear like Houdini. They'll

64

never know. They're going to take at least five minutes to get here. They'll think I'm cowering under a desk, or gone down to the General Science workshops.

They'll search and they'll search. When they don't find me under the desk or in the general work area, they'll try to figure it out. They'll rerun the CCTV. They'll never stop. *Hack into the CCTV, Anton. Shut that down.* They'll know I'm in the ceilings. I gulp down huge trembling gales of air. I try to stop my heart racing, try to stop panic freezing my mind.

Surely somebody will rescue us soon? Surely they will? I pray they will. I pray the SAS will storm the building. Send in a SWAT team. I pray Anton will release Lock Down. Maybe he can figure out something with carbon dioxide. Without burning us alive. I got to get to a safe place. I got to call them myself. Shout at them. Beg them. Plead with them. Let them know. Maybe they don't really believe Gilly.

I try to tell myself, don't stress. Markel and Jase won't figure nothing out. They're too stupid. They won't rerun shit. They're too lazy. I want to climb into the ceiling straight away. But there's something I got to do first. I got about four minutes now. I got to check on Aliesha and Kady. I got to find out what happened in Lab One.

I'm flying, darting down benches, skirting shelving,

65

trying hard not to touch nothing, not to topple no book and leave no one page fluttering to give me away. The address system's died. It really is dead for keeps. But they know where I've gone. I try to work out what they'll do. Will they try to take over the whole science block? Will they man the corridor outside and start searching from both ends? Suddenly I skid to a halt. If they do that then I'm not only running away from them, *I'm running towards them too*.

Get out now, I'm screaming at myself. Get out and hide. But Lab One is only just up ahead. Forget Lab One. I turn back to race for the last tech den. I'm going to ground. But in that split second, when I stop, when I decide to hide, when I turn, I hear a low moan.

*Someone is still alive in Lab One.*

*And I've drawn the shooters back.*

Everything in me is screaming: hide, run, turn, hide, run, turn, but I'm not going to leave anyone like I left Ruby again. So I don't turn. Instead I race like I've never done before, through the lab, through the next tech den, into Lab One.

It's a mess.

Miss Carter is still lying there. She still looks surprised. The blood around her is turning black. I search the floor, looking for Aliesha. Looking for Kady. There's no Kady.

She must still be alive. She must be down in the gym. But behind the back bench is Aliesha. She's still alive too. A huge rush of relief sweeps through me. Then it's blown away by fear. She's alive. How can I keep her alive? She's wounded. Badly. She's dragged herself to the back. Her face is gone. I can't look at it. I must look at it. I force myself over towards her. She moans.

'Ali,' I say.

Ali don't say nothing at first.

Finally she says something, but it don't sound like proper words. I bend nearer. 'Lee?' she says. But she can't see me, because something's happened to her face and her eyes are gone.

She starts whimpering. And I'm thinking, what now? Run, hide, leave her? You can't do nothing else. Instead, I pull a glass beaker off the desk. I race to the side sinks. My heart is pounding so hard. I fill it up. Ruby wanted water and I couldn't give her any. I race back to her. I say, 'Sip this.' I place it in her hand. I tighten her poor bloodied hand around it. I say, 'Just sip it, Ali, and don't make no noise. And if they come back, play dead. Play dead, do you hear me? If anyone comes back, play dead.'

She moans. I ain't sure she got all that.

There's no time to be gentle.

'I'm going to help you, Ali, but not now.'

67

She tries to nod. That's gross. I can't look at her. She's whimpering. 'Ali,' I say, now really cross and all. 'You shut up. If they hear you, they're going to kill you. You shut the frick up, you hear me? And I'll come back. If you don't shut up, I'm going to leave you.'

'Lee,' she says, all blood frothing at her face. 'Don't leave me.'

'Then shut up and play dead.'

'I'm sorry about Carl.'

I stop, my mind a blank. Carl? Then it all floods back. Carl. The pictures on the Internet. The messages. Me and Carl photo-digitally altered so that you'd think the worst. What a laugh. Ha ha.

'I'm sorry.'

'Shut up and play dead,' I hiss.

'I'm sorry.'

So it was Aliesha after all.

'I was angry . . .' her voice splutters. 'I was jealous.' A dribble of blood foams around her chin. 'I'm sorry . . . I thought if Carl and you . . .' She can't catch her breath. 'You're a good person, Lee.' She clutches out at me.

I ain't got time for this.

'We was friends . . .'

'I'm going to help you,' I say. 'Quit worrying. Now, lie still.'

'OK,' she says, and places her mangled face on the floor and lies there.

Now I can go.

And I do go. I race to the tech den. I'm happy it's the one Anton and me messed up when we first got out, because I don't have time to do this carefully. I scramble up on to the work bench using the shelves like a ladder. I climb. I lift out the polystyrene square above me and I hoist myself up, and I don't even notice the pain in my shoulders or the weight of my body or nothing. And my blood is racing so fast I don't notice anything until I'm lying face down on the joists with that ceiling tile placed exactly back in its slot. And then I feel my heart and it's like an engine pumping.

Like a machine gun firing.

# 11.25 a.m.
## Friday, 18 September

I lie there. I don't move. I don't do nothing. I lie there
and wait. I shut my eyes. I keep seeing Aliesha's face. I
can't do this any more. My chest is quivering like badly
set jelly. I got to wipe her face out. I got to think of
something else. Think of something else, I order myself.
Stop thinking about her face. About the nose what ain't
there any more, how she must've turned sideways as the
bullet ripped it off, ripped out an eye. I got to stop
thinking. Remember this morning. Remember something
before all this.

I remember.

It's like another country.

Me in the kitchen mad at Connor.

Sally biting her nails. I slap her fingers away from her
mouth. I growl at her. Sally looks like she's going to start
crying. One look from me stops all that. I know it's not fair.
None of it's fair. It's not fair on Sally. It's not fair on me. I

70

*shouldn't have to do Fridays. Friday is my day when I go to Young Carers' Club and today is special. Today they're selecting the Young Carers' X Factor, and Miss X Factor Last Year is visiting. I'm trying out for it.*

*I was trying out for it.*

*I sing. Nobody ever taught me. I just do it. When I sing people stop and listen. Sometimes they cry. My voice has got a kind of power over them. The kind of power I never have at any other time. I like it. It makes me feel strong.*

*I am supposed to be singing tonight at the Young Carers' X Factor, which is sad and lame and nothing like the real X Factor, but for me it's as good as it gets. I'm not supposed to be taking Sally to school, or picking Sally up from Latchkey Club, or making Sally supper, or babysitting Sally all evening, because it's Friday and Friday is my day.*

*And Miss X Factor Last Year is visiting.*

*At least, we invited her.*

Eventually they come. I figure they were waiting in the corridor outside, but when I didn't show they came in to search. How many of them are there? Is it Markel and Jase and Lucas again? I don't know who it is, because there's no crack for me to see through.

What if it's Connor?

What if I had a gun and it was Connor. If he was

71

alone? If it could save Aliesha?

Would I?

I listen. I think there's two of them. I don't know their voices. I wait and I wait and I know I'm waiting to hear a gunshot, to hear they killed Aliesha. No gunshot comes. I nod to myself in the darkness; she's playing dead all right. Good old Aliesha, maybe she's not such a loser. Maybe she really is dead.

I'd like to think I would kill him if it would save everyone.

But could I? If it *could* save everyone?

Good old Aliesha. We're going to beat them. We're going to outwit them. And for a minute it's like a game, but it ain't no game.

And that's funny, because they think it is. They're talking to themselves like they're the army on a mission. I listen.

VOICE 1: Checking out Lab One. Over. Two dead. Over. Suspect still at large. Over.

Whoever it is sounds like they're pretending they got a walkie-talkie. They're so stupid. But then I'm surprised, because I'm wrong, because I hear a crackle. I hear a voice that can only be coming from a handset.

VOICE 2 FROM A HANDSET:   Search and destroy. Over.

| | |
|---|---|
| VOICE 1: | Copied. Over. |
| VOICE 2 FROM A HANDSET: | Any luck? Over. |
| VOICE 3: | Say Nope. |
| VOICE 1: | OK. Nope. Over. Searching forward to Lab Two and beyond [like they're going to search outer space next]. Over. |
| VOICE 2 FROM A HANDSET: | Good job. Over. |

They're talking like they're in a computer game. Where did they get walkie-talkies from? How come? That takes planning. That takes money and organisation. I don't think anyone in YOU OP 78 has got money or organisation, least of all Damian's gang.

I lie there, my heart thumping and thumping. I'm thinking and thinking. That this – all this – the guns and the kids and the walkie-talkies are all part of something I don't understand.

Is Damian that psycho? Did he sit at home with Psycho Sam and dream up a real-life computer game to play out in the corridors of this school? And even if he did – because he'd probably *like* to do that – even if he did, where did he get the money from? And I know I don't know nothing about money and how you get it if you ain't got a job – and nobody's folks have got jobs these days. I know there are other ways of getting money. But even if they could get it that way: let's say he got the money – let's say he scammed it off the Web, or broke into a bloody bank – where did he get the guns, that many guns? Cos these days, since the riots, since Stop and Search went totally mental and became Stop and Arrest and Stop and Imprison and Stop and Grass Up All Your Mates, and Stop and Get Your Face on *Name & Shame*, Get Your Whole Life on *Crimewatch*, nobody can get guns and keep it quiet for long.

I give up thinking about it. I don't know nothing. Seems like the tougher the government gets, the more it's teaching morons like Damian to get sneakier. I don't know. But that means they're just going to bust out in nastier ways.

There's a lot of kids in on this. I lie there in the darkness and I try to figure out how many kids. And I count on my fingers and come up with at least seven. They've got to be the most stupidest seven kids in the school. If I lie here a bit longer I'll be able to work out exactly who they are. So I lie there in the darkness, making my list of kids. But every which way I count, Connor is always one of them.

I jolt back into reality.

*'Check the tech dens,' says a voice.*

There's the sound of something knocked into, kicked over.

I freeze.

*'Someone's been here,' says the voice.*

My heart starts up an irregular beat. It pounds in my ears.

I lie trying to listen to every crack and creak going on. I try to figure out if they're there, below me, if they've moved along to the next tech den, or are outside on the science corridor, or if they're waiting for me to come out just as patiently as I'm waiting for them to go away.

There's a slight squeak, like trainers on a plastic floor. *They're still there!*

*Please, someone rescue me. Please.* The police have got to come. They must have had zillions of calls by now. I'm sure I can hear a helicopter. I'm sure that's a helicopter hovering low over the building. Have they landed? Where have they landed? If they've landed on the Olympic-turf there's no way they can get in through the front main entrance. The Lock Down there is serious. Continuous high voltage, three grille-gated portals, the last one with solid metal electrocuted sheeting.

Someone *is* waiting. *Right below me.* I'm sure I can hear breathing.

They've got to get in. They've got to get in and save

me. I listen for the sound of some distant explosion. Maybe they've got in another way? Maybe they're creeping around through the school. I start worrying that they might mistake me for one of the killers and shoot me, which is stupid, but when you're half frightened out of your mind it's the kind of thing you think.

Then I work out the SWAT team won't shoot Aliesha, because of her face and all that. So I lie still to see if I can hear anyone helping her in the next room. But I don't hear a thing except the soft clicky buzz of my comm and I know a text message has come through. But I'm lying here so frightened and so quiet, I don't try to struggle over on to my side to get my comm out – even though it might be Connor.

Surely they must have gone. Is it safe to move? Nobody can stay still for that long – not Jase and them anyway. I flex an ankle. I got to move too. I can't hold this position any longer. But is it safe? Think of something else. Explore the ceiling above you. It's a pretty tight squash. I can't move much. There's some concrete decking just above my head. Somewhere over by my feet is a gap like a trapdoor with no trap in it. Maybe it leads upwards on to the concrete decking above.

I lift my foot up, very slowly. It don't hit no trapdoor. I can feel cool air over my shin. Maybe it's some kind of way to get up to A level. Maybe it's a shaft, a service shaft over the science wing? My heart starts up. If there's a service shaft it might go anywhere. It might go everywhere!

Suddenly my hopes are up; my imagination is up too. *Of course* it *must* be a service shaft. The maintenance team have got to fix stuff, haven't they? I bet everything needs fixing, all the time, because everyone knows YOU OP kids are stupid and destroy stuff.

Please let it be a service shaft.

I listen. The helicopter has gone. If it *was* a helicopter. I can't hold this position much longer. My legs ache, my tummy aches, my arms are so tense they set up a tremble. Shaking sets in. I mustn't move. I'm going to break something. Where the hell are the Special Weapons And Tactics guys? If I can work out where this service shaft goes and how to navigate it, if I can find a way to get Aliesha up here with me . . . My imagination mushrooms. Maybe Anton too. Maybe there *is* a way out from these shafts, one nobody knows about. One that ain't Locked Down.

I raise my foot again, just flexing it – just trying to probe the shaft entrance.

But my leg is trembling. I can't stop it trembling.

It won't stop.

I knock a tile. It shudders. It pops from its setting. Right out.

77

# 11.42 a.m.
## Friday, 18 September

There's nobody there.

Nobody's listening.

Nobody's waiting to put a bullet into me.

They've gone.

I heave a sigh of relief. I move at last. I swivel round. My arms are so stiff. I use my cell comm as a torch. I look to see if the service shaft can do all the things I'm hoping it can. And I'm not wrong. Somewhere over the middle of the tech den the shaft ends. It slopes to just about a metre above the ceiling tiles and there are rungs and a rail there. If I get down – like out of the ceiling – and mark the tile under the shaft exit, I can remove it and get back directly into the shaft itself.

So I do it. I lift up the tile that popped. I pull it right out and place it beside me. I peer through. It's a three-metre drop to the floor. Peanuts. I position the tile so that when I drop it will plop back into place. I swing out and let my legs slide first. I dangle myself by my arms until my feet are only about a metre and a half from the floor. I let go. The floor jars as I hit. My legs buckle at the knee but I don't make any noise. I'm not going to neither.

I mark the tile below the service shaft. It ain't hard: it's got MAINTENANCE stencilled across it.

Now I got to figure out how to get Aliesha up into the shaft. It won't be easy. Even if she can still see with one eye, I don't think she's going to feel like opening it. Can she do it blind? I think about that. If I don't get her into that shaft before those kids come back she won't need to play dead again. But how to do it? Suddenly I'm struck by a horror that the shooters *are going* to come. They'll come because they know I'm still here. *In fact, they're coming already* . . . I start shaking again. If I'm going to help Aliesha I got to do it now.

I hear something. It's like cheering, but it's coming from far away. I crouch and listen. My heart lurches with hope. The rescue team? But then the windows start rattling and there's that telltale popping noise. It ain't no rescue team. They're shooting again. The air smells stale – of spent sparklers, of dry smoke. It's gunshot.

I wonder who they're shooting at. I wonder if it's Connor. What if shooting Connor could save everyone? Save me, save Ruby, save Anton. Would I wish it was him? I dare myself to wish it, a proper eyes-squeezed-tight wish. It's only a wish, for frick's sake.

I taste blood in my mouth. I just bit my lip. Then I tell myself to stop it, stop listening to the guns. My legs unlock. I'm moving. Lab One. My heart's in my throat. I get down by Aliesha. She ain't dead, although she's pale and all that. She's moaning, 'No, no.' I catch her bloodied hand. I say, 'It ain't them, it's me, Ali. I'm going to get you somewhere safe where they can't find you. I'm going to look at your face and patch you up.'

She grabs on to my hand so hard my knuckles all crunch together.

I try not to look at her face. I don't want to lose my nerve. Her face ain't pretty like it was before. I pick up the beaker of water that I left beside her. It's empty. I cross to the sinks and fill it up very quietly. I think there ain't going to be a lot of water up there in the service shaft. I hastily gulp down the water myself. I look around to see if anyone's left a water bottle or canteen around and I'm in luck. Somebody's bag that was left on the floor has split open and spilled out all its stuff. There's a water canteen with YOU OP 78 on it and the school logo. I pick it up. I go back to the sink and fill it and stuff it in my waistband.

I crouch down by Aliesha again. But I'm getting

in the book cupboard, are gone.

There is screaming coming from the science wing. It gets louder. I see two kids running down the corridor. I don't wait to see what they're running from. I move out of sight, clamber up over the dictionaries and the reference books and struggle up balancing on *Modern Art Movements in Germany* and lift up the ceiling tile. I flop it back like I'm already an expert at getting in and out of ceilings. I hoist myself up with my trembling arms. I only hold on to the joists. I drag my legs in after. I swivel round and pick up the ceiling tile and position it back in its place. I lie trembling over the polystyrene listening to shots coming down the corridor. POP. POW. The sound of running feet stops. The thud of something heavy hitting the flooring and scudding into the wall.

*I lie there over the polystyrene tiles, listening to the thud and scud, remembering how I woke up; how I woke up thinking: It's not my day.*

*It's not my day to drop off Sally.*

*It's not my day to pick her up.*

*I was thinking: Connor knows this. Sally knows this. Everybody knows Monday, Tuesday, Wednesday and Thursday are my days. Not Fridays.*

*It's Connor on Fridays. He knows it is. And I make sure he* does. 'It's your turn today, you selfish, lazy bastard,' I yell. I'm so flipping fed up. But I get Sally ready anyway.

I pump some mush or other into her. I give her a slug of milk and wipe her face. She tries to hurry, because she knows she's wasting my time. She knocks the glass of milk on the floor. I scream at her. I call her a bloody stupid retard. But I clean it up anyway. I shove a packet of crisps (mine, that I'd bought for me for today), a cold turkey nugget and two leftover crust ends from a long-finished loaf into a plastic bag. I stick it in her backpack. 'That's for after school,' I say. 'If you eat it before Latchkey Club, it's your fault.'

I pack my school bag. I got my Five Minutes of Fame and Fortune forms to file. I got to submit them before the weekend. No time now. I'll do it later. Maybe online at school.

I check on Mum. She is lying staring at the wall, so everything's OK. I don't ask her if she needs anything, because I don't have time to sort her out. I dither by the bed. I give up and go and bang on the bathroom door. 'I bloody hate you.'

I mean it. I hate Connor.

'Fridays are your days.' And he spends so long in there I'm not able to shower or nothing. He don't even say sorry.

'It's not my day,' I yell.

But it is – isn't it? Connor made me late, and now I'm here listening to the thud and scud. Did he do that on purpose?

Is Connor in with them?

44

jumpy. I want to be back in those service shafts. 'C'mon, Ali,' I say. 'Sip it. You got to drink. Don't give up. They can rebuild your face, make you much prettier than you ever was and all for free. But you got to stay alive — you hear me?' She does hear me, but I guess she's in pain or shock or something. She's even more scared stupid than I am.

Least she manages to take something. Most of it gets spilled on the floor. I start worrying that if they come back to check, they're going to see water spilled there. But I stop worrying. Worry don't do no good. If it's those dumbsters, Jase and Lucas, they ain't never going to work out that some water got spilled because I tried to give it to Ali. They just going to say, 'Oh look, there's water on the floor,' and that's all.

'Can you stand?' I say.

Aliesha ain't sure. She ain't confident. So I tell her, 'I'm going to be here, so you can lean on me.' But she still ain't sure. I don't know what to say to change that. I know it ain't right of me but I say, 'If you don't get up an' try, Ali, I'm getting out and you can stay put if that's all you want to do. They can come back and kill you for all the frick I care.'

A shudder goes through her and she looks like she's going to scream. If it wasn't for all that blood all over her face I'd have clapped my hand across her mouth like a shot. But instead I say, 'Don't scream neither.'

So she takes my hand and tries to pull herself up. I'm trembling too and the windows start rattling again. I hold on to her and say, 'Ali, we got to move quickly. I don't want to leave you again.'

She whimpers, 'Don't leave me, Lee, please.' But the windows is rattling and rattling. She's all bubbling blood where she's trying to beg me, so I say, 'I ain't going to leave you but you got to hurry.'

Ali staggers to her feet. I hold her. She's weak enough to fall the minute I let go. I'm shaking, but a little bit of shaking ain't going to stop me. I've made up my mind to save her. I hold on to the sides of benches and worktops and chair backs and I half stumble, half drag and half lift Aliesha until we get across the floor.

We're nearly at the door to the tech den when the windows stop rattling. That worries me more than the rattling, because that means the killers aren't in the gym any more or, if they are, they're being all quiet and they're listening. I got to be very quiet now too. They haven't forgotten about me. They still want to get me. I whisper to Aliesha, 'You've got to be really strong now. You've got to be really brave. I'm going to get you up into the ceilings, and you're going to do it without screaming and stuff. You're going to do it quick. You're going to do every damn thing I say, and then you're going to be OK.'

And she says, 'OK.'

Her voice is all small like she's a tiny kid and is going to behave herself. I breathe a sigh of relief. She must be in shed loads of pain and she's usually the screamy type, so I know she's serious now.

We get into the tech den and I move her to the centre floor space until she's exactly under the right tile. I look at her. I think, *How the hell am I going to get her up there?*

She just stands and waits, all patient. If she could see, she'd be just looking at me, but I've wrapped my jacket over her face to stop the blood drips giving us away.

'Stay put, Ali.' I place her hand on a chair back so she can steady herself. I drag out the specimens display unit and I take her other hand and help her feel across the top of the unit so she knows how big it is. 'You're going to climb up on to that, Ali,' I say.

She starts to raise up a leg. I make a saddle stirrup step out of my two hands and put it beneath her foot. I say, 'You got to do as I say.'

She says, 'Yes.'

'Put your weight on my hands and use it like a step.'

She ain't sure, but she does it. I haul her a bit. She

drags herself a bit. 'Stretch out in front and balance on the wall,' I say. We get her up on to the specimen box. She steadies herself on the wall. I look at her and I'm so sorry, but I can't afford to be sorry, can I?

Aliesha moans. I can see she's really unsteady, but I don't take it. There'll be time for all that moaning later, so I get really harsh. 'You do as I say, Ali, or I'll leave you for the killers, and they ain't going to be helping you step on no hands.'

She whimpers and tries to turn her head. The jacket I stuck round her poor face is all flappy and bloodstained and suddenly right there and then I feel like puking up. But I get all harsh on myself too. I ain't going to puke and leave a smell and a mess for those stupid Year Nine idiots to track me down with. Instead I grab her legs and I say, 'Stand straight, Ali. Try and think of this like doing bar work in the gym. Just let go of the wall and stand steady, and then I'm going to make another stirrup cup out of my hands and you're going to step in it. You're going to bounce yourself up into the air, and if you don't, I'm going to leave you.'

She's shaking and trembling, but I know she can do it. The opening into the shaft ain't that far above her now, and if she can flop into it and on to that slope, it's firm enough to take her. There's rungs on the side of it too. I can shove her up from below, and she can claw her way up hanging on to them.

I tell her if I leave her they're going to cut off her legs and laugh while they're doing it. I say, 'How're you going to like that, Ali?'

She's so scared, she just whimpers. I pinch her leg and say, 'You felt that? Now you imagine them sawing away, and how long they're going to take with the cutting, and all. All you've got to do is bounce a little and push up and flop forward and hang on.' My voice has got this edge in it because I'm starting to get very scared. They really *are* going to come back. I'm thinking, *Why the hell am I bothering with Aliesha?* Soon the police will be here and it'll all be over. Except that now I've started bothering with her, I'm damned if I'm going to give up on her, even if she's whimpering and a big loser and all that.

So I don't. I pinch her leg again. She stands straight. I climb on to the counter beside her.

I hiss, 'Raise one foot.'

She raises up her foot and tries to balance herself on one leg. Suddenly I think, *What if she can't do it?* But I stop thinking like that, because she *is* going to do it.

I cup my hands into a stirrup. I guide her foot into it. I say now in a different voice, 'You're on the edge of the trampoline, Ali. There's no chair to stand on to get up.

85

You're going to bounce on my hands. I'm going to give you a leg-up. You're going to bounce with all your might, because you've only got one go at this. When you're flying through the air, you're going to stretch out your hands and hook them on to anything whether it hurts you or not, then you flop forward and you ain't going to scream. OK?'

I think she nods. I'm not looking. I ain't taking no for no answer so I say, 'OK: one, two, three, go.'

Aliesha bounces. It's a half-hearted timid sort of bounce that won't save her, unless I do something. I push up with all my might. I catch her legs together. I hold her. She's trying to sink back down, but I say, 'Oh no, you don't.' I shove her up again and hiss, 'To your right, feel the rungs, catch them, hold them, pull yourself up.'

Her hand is waving around like she's drowning, but I snap at her. Her hand closes round a strut and at least it's one hand, but she knocks the ceiling tile clean off and it comes crashing down. I don't know whether to let go of her and catch it, because if it breaks then our getaway is busted. I don't let go of her. The ceiling tile dips across the tech lab like some flipping frisbee and knocks bottles clean off the shelf. They're glass bottles. I know before they even hit the ground they're going to break, they're going to make one helluva din. The entire school's going to hear them.

I shove on Liesha's legs even harder. She's got a grip on the rungs now. She flops forward. Slowly, painfully, she hauls herself up into the ventilation shaft. I only take my hands off her when I can't reach her no more. Her legs are disappearing up into the ceiling.

The ceiling tile didn't break but I can hear the windows rattling in a different way, and they always do that when someone is smacking through the corridor fire doors and running down The Crossing on B corridor like demons from hell are after them.

Like lightning I kick the broken glass from the toppled bottles under the benches. I drag off my T-shirt. I race into Lab One. I wipe the floor. I wipe up the faint smear of blood that gives us away. Then I race back into the tech lab, back to the open tile under the ventilation shaft, back to Aliesha clinging in there. I grab up the dropped tile. I stand on the specimen box. I replace the tile.

'Stay quiet,' I hiss at Aliesha.

The windows are rattling like crazy. I ain't got time. I know somebody's sprinting towards us. It's too late for me to try and get back up into the ceiling. I crouch down behind the benches and try to tell my heart not to beat, not to give me away. I'm silenter than any mouse crouched in any hole ever.

And they bust into the lab. The windows are rattling so hard I can tell just by the vibrations exactly where they are. There in Lab One – but they ain't really looking, because I don't hear none of them say, 'So where's Aliesha's body gone to?' They just walking and kicking out at things and I'm cowering.

Dear God, please don't let them find me.

# 12.04 p.m.
## Friday, 18 September

One of them kicks at something. I hear it rattle across the floor, then he speaks. It's Jase again. I steady my breath. If those two idiots find me I'm dead. I cower back into the space under the desk, trying to tell my heart to shut up.

'What we looking for anyway?' says Jase.

'Dunno,' says Markel – must be Markel.

'What they gonna do with all those kids then?' says Jase, all conversational.

Markel laughs. 'Strawberry jam,' he says.

'All of 'em?' says Jase, like he'd like to salvage a few as a trophy.

'Boom,' says Markel.

You know, I never noticed it before, but Markel often speaks like that. You know: 'strawberry jam, boom, crash, pow', like he spent his entire life watching cartoons.

'Whaddya mean?' says Jase. 'Boom what?'

'Boom. Boom. Boom,' says Markel.

They're in the tech den now. I cross my fingers. I close my eyes. My heart is thudding so loud I'm sure the floor's going to vibrate.

'They gonna boom them all?' says Jase.

I can tell from the sudden excitement in his voice he thinks that's a really fun idea.

Markel grunts.

'That'll bloody teach them,' says Jase, although what he wants to teach them he don't say. And it's not like they'll learn much if they're all dead anyway. But my heart is going even worse, because Connor is down there with those kids. He was in the hall when the whole thing started. And if he ain't one of them, then he'll be boomed too. If he is one of them, I don't know which is worse: to be innocent and dead, or alive and guilty. I squeeze my eyes tight.

'How they gonna do that then?' says Jase. He kicks at more stuff. I hear glass beakers falling on the floor and breaking. I'm glad, because that'll disguise the bits of glass I missed. And then I'm not glad in case he bends down to pick them up. But I know he ain't going to do that, but my chest is trembling – what if he did? He don't though, because he's too lazy. I remember with a sickening lurch how he just shot through those tables in the library. He was too lazy to bend down. I think of

90

Ruby alone in that dark cupboard. I think of Aliesha up there. I'm praying like frick she don't whimper.

'Fireworks,' says Markel.

And I wonder what he means. So does Jase.

'Like bonfire night and stuff?' he asks.

I suppose Markel has nodded, because Jase continues, 'Wonder if Damian gonna let me light the fuse.'

The fuse? Did I miss something? What fuse?

And for once Jase is one step ahead of me. They haven't wired the whole place, have they?

Jase continues, 'When're they gonna boom them all up?' Like he's talking about a football final or a Fame and Fortune Fone-in.

'Dunno, do I,' says Markel, which must be the longest sentence he's managed in a while.

Jase suddenly stops. I can see his boots centimetres from my nose. 'Wouldn't that be funny,' he says with a strange chuckle. 'Booming all those kids up right in front of their parents and the telly seeing it all, so if you missed seeing your kid's head fly off you could watch it on rerun.'

He starts to laugh a real belly laugh like that is so the funniest joke anyone ever thought up. He moves a few centimetres forward. My heart is going so hard I think I'm going to faint. Markel throws something else on the floor. I see in the reflection of the glass cabinet door Jase raise his hand and grab hold of Markel. He looks around nervously and then he drops his voice to a whisper, as if there are hidden microphones recording everything. 'Where're we gonna be?'

Markel stops at that. He hesitates. 'Dunno,' he says. But his voice has a different tone. Something cunning has entered it. He gives a sly little cough.

And maybe all these years I've been underestimating Jase, because he says, 'Are you gonna do it?'

And in the reflection in the glass cabinet, I can see the two of them exchange a look. Then they whisper.

'You do it and we'll get the hell out,' whispers Jase.

Jase may be smarter than I thought, but he's missed the new note in Markel's cough. He don't know Markel has his own plan. His own little deal.

Markel don't say nothing except, 'Lock Down.'

The two of them leave. I stay there catching my breath, trying to take in this new threat. And I can't get my head round it. They got guns and maybe they got grenades? And they're going to blow us all up right in front of everyone? At least, Markel thinks so, even if Jase don't know nothing about it.

I don't get it. I don't get why Markel and Jase ain't on the same page. What's it all about then? I don't get why they're doing it. I don't understand nothing, not even if it is mental, not even if they're so seriously disturbed they need brain surgery, except that I do understand something: it's a lot worse than I thought.

When the shaking stops, I pray like crazy Anton can hack into Lock Down. I pray the service shaft's got its own exit. I pray the SWAT team's going to get here soon. But I just carry on with the old plan, because that's the only thing I got. Get to a safe place. Call out. Tell them to get me out quick.

And I pray my comm battery don't die on me.

Maybe they're just joking about the fireworks.

Connor. My mind goes blank, like what shall I do about Connor now? I don't know nothing about grenades. What were they chucking that time in the library? I ain't even very good at science. How do grenades work actually? How long have I got? But even if my mind is blank my brain is working. It's figuring things out. Even as I'm climbing back up the science shelves and lifting out the ceiling panel and hauling myself in and replacing the tile so carefully nobody's going to know anything; my brain is calculating: get on to the police, tell them, get them to get a hand-grenade disposal expert in. I stop and mentally curl up into a little ball at the thought. I wish I was six again, like Sally, and somebody else was here and not me.

It's Ali what pulls me out of myself. 'Lee,' she whispers in that new voice of hers carved out of a half-empty face.

'I'm here,' I hiss back. 'I'm coming.'

I start the slow process of lifting and hauling myself across the tiles from joist strut to joist strut, until I'm under the lip of the service shaft. I wriggle round on to my back and twist myself into a crazy hairpin and struggle up into the shaft. Up the rungs, up the slope, on to the little level landing. I end up lying there right beside her, panting and panting.

But I don't lie there long. 'C'mon,' I say, after I got my breath back. 'We got to get up into the main bit of the shaft. When we're there, I'll take a look at your face and you can sleep. I'll give you water.'

'Thanks, Lee,' she says. 'I knew you was my friend.'

My throat catches at that. I bite my lip. But I don't say nothing, even though my heart could bust just looking at her. And I don't act sorry for her neither. I couldn't stand it if she got weepy. I ain't going to get weepy. So I just poke her and say, 'C'mon then.'

Safe in the service shaft, I don't worry about no windows rattling, nor guns popping. I break sweat. A nice kind of Thank God sweat. I listen anyway though, because there's a different kind of noise, a faint buzzing, like a helicopter is out over the place. I pray to God it is. It must be them.

I shove and coax and bully Aliesha further up the service tunnel. We find this place where it opens out on a bit of a landing, bigger than the last one. I reckon this is the best place. It's a kind of junction of service shafts. There's just about enough room to lie down side by side. It's flat and best of all there's a skylight higher up. That's a big help. The light shines straight down through a small plastic panel in the outer roof. If I lie on my back and squint, I can just make out the shadow of something moving around way out there in the blue sky. Bet it's that helicopter. Bet it's on its way to help us.

At last I pull out my phone.

Seven messages.

One by one I open them.

# 12.25 p.m.
## Friday, 18 September

Inbox:

**GILLY:** I've called the police. They r very worried about u stay where u are. I'll let your mum no. I'll pick up Sally. Can I give your number out? There's people who want to know what's happening. Gilly

**UNKNOWN:** This is Tilda's mum. Gillian Potts gave me your number. Is Tilda all right? Please tell her to call me. I'm so worried. Thank you Tina Strickland

**MARCIE:** Babes – I just heard on the news – it's bad are you OK? Marcie

**ANTON:** I took out the intercom. Still working on Lock Down. My way.

**UNKNOWN:** Where are you Leah Jackson? Where ever you are we're going to find you. Mwhahahah.

I don't answer none of those communications except Anton. I send him a happy face and three words.

**CCTV. Your way.**

Nothing from Connor. Nothing from Mum.

I don't shut down my comm. While I got some battery left, I need to call the police, the army, whoever it takes to get me out. A vague, wild hope starts building in my

96

head. I imagine them sending a wire down through that little plastic window, right down to me, with a neat little seat and a neat little harness. I strap myself on to that little seat.

I stop dreaming. I punch in 999 and wait. I go through the usual automated choices and get put through to a lady. She's on my visuals, way before she sees my call. When she plugs into me I'm almost hyperventilating. 'Please,' I whisper. I hadn't realised how scared I sound, how hopelessly small my voice is. How my words whisper up and around and echo in a weird way. Christ, I'm scared. I'm so scared I stop speaking and my words just won't come out. I feel my heart pounding and pounding on my ribs, like they're made of thin plastic and they're going to fracture at anything.

'Yes,' she says all sassy and like: so don't waste my time with whatever it is you've got to tell me.

'Please,' I squeak. 'You got to help us. I'm in YOU OP 78. There's been shooting. They've got guns.' At the words 'shootings' and 'guns' I can hear the surveillance taps click in and I know I got her attention.

'What's your name?' she clacks out.

'They've got all the kids in the gym. They've shot my friend Aliesha and there's a girl in the book cupboard. She might be dead by now.'

'What's your name?' she clacks out again.

'Leah,' I whisper. 'I'm Leah Jackson, YOU OP student category 5 number 3445.'

'Just a moment,' she says. She puts me on hold. I see her getting up my details.

'Leah Jackson? 89 Ludgate House, Ellerfield Estates?'

'Yes,' I whisper.

'Where are you, Leah?' she says. Her voice ain't kind, just brisk and businesslike, as if it's quite normal to have kids shooting each other up every day of the week. 'I'm going to put you on hold, Leah, while I search for your GPS.'

'My GPS?' I whisper, but she's put me on hold already, before I can tell her that the satellite GPS system don't work on my cell comm, that my comm is old – that it's *so* old I'm worried about my batteries. I touch in the Leave A Voicemail App. I whisper, 'Please, I'll call back. I want to check if my brother's OK.' And I do. I suddenly want to check on him so much.

I hang up, hoping like hell she'll get the message. Like there's a whole bunch of crazy kids killing each other all around me; she *has* to do something.

I go to call Connor. I stop. What if they took his comm? What if they won't let him answer? What if he's hiding and my call gives him away? I want to call him so bad. I want to be really sure it ain't him. He's not one of the ones shooting at me – is he?

But I don't call. I'm too scared.

I text him instead. I know Connor's only got a shitty old comm, which can't do nothing fancy or nice like he'd like it to. But it gets texts. If he's not one of them, they won't hear nothing. If he is, he could still let me know something. So I text. I write: **You ok? Connor? What's up?**

I want to write: I'm safe I'm in the ceilings and I've called the police and they're going to winch me up through the roof in a little seat strapped to a harness, so if you are one of Damian's gang try and get out or something, because they're going to shoot to kill – but I don't, because I don't know who's going to read that text. It could be anyone and I can't give nothing away.

And moreover even if nobody got his comm, I know the truth and it hurts.

I don't trust him.

If he is one of them he might tell. He might come after me himself. I wouldn't put it past him to shoot me – boom – just like that. Especially if Damian said so.

I think about that – if he *was* one of them, and if he *did* come after me and if I had a gun, would I shoot back?

It's a question I wish I knew the answer to.

But before I get a reply from Connor, my comm goes again. It's an imaging comm with all the extras, or it would be an imaging comm with all the extras if only my comm supported all the extras. But even though it's not as shitty a comm as Connor's – on account of the fact that I don't throw it across the room every time I lose at War Game, it still can't support the full imaging, so instead I just get the head of the speaker. It's weird, this head is just floating in space in front of me. It ain't even his real head. It's one of those cartoon photo-fit heads like in an ID kit. It's got a stupid moustache and impossibly thick spectacles, like who even wears spectacles these days anyway? I know it's not the real person – just a download. Anyway, it says:

'Hi, this is your personal Crime Reduction Negotiator, Commander Peterson, calling. Am I speaking to Miss Leah Jackson?'

I nod my head. He continues, his eyes rolling around my hiding space in a scan and record motion.

'We are so sorry to have kept you waiting. Can you confirm your identity? What is your post code?'

I tell him.

'Your call is very important to us; we are unable to locate your exact position to enact evacuation procedures.' It pauses and I'm beginning to think I'm talking to a machine. Then it starts again:

'Would you please activate your locator?'

'I can't,' I say. 'My GPS locator is bust. I can't activate it.' I hang my head in frustration. Why should my locator be bust – right when I need it most? Sometimes I think the universe has jinxed me. Of all the bleeding apps on the comm to get broken and just when it's probably life and death. I glance at Aliesha briefly. Probably death. She's lying so quiet. I shove her a little, very gently, with my elbow. She stirs and twitches. She's alive.

'Please,' I start. 'You've got to get me out. I can't tell you where I am, because I crawled a long way and I got my friend with me and she's hurt bad – and it's Aliesha Mulholland. Please, you've got to help us.'

'Can you give us your exact location?' asks the negotiator like I didn't just explain all that. 'Have you tried the position app?'

'Can't you release Lock Down?' I say. They've got to be able to do that. Since the riots, since the Civic Disorder Bill, when the government prioritised the safety of public buildings, Lock Down went remote. We had a security officer come in and do an assembly on it. During a riot, at the touch of a screen, from the safety of their station, the police can secure every government building right across the country. They've got to be able to release it the same way, surely?

'Negative,' says the head. 'Once internal Lock Down is triggered, it overrides remote access. Have you tried your position app?'

'It don't work. Nothing bloody works on my comm. You're coming through with only your head.' I start to get a tone in my voice like I'm going to cry or something. I bite my lip. I can't cry. The universe ain't got nothing to do with this. My comm is crap, because I come from a crap family with no money, and a sad mum who ain't up to it, and the government don't reckon to pay crap families to have comms that work. It's not like when every flipping kid had a BlackBerry no matter how poor they was. Back then everyone talked about 'relative poverty' like real poverty was the thing left behind in the dark ages.

'The comm don't work,' I say flatly.

'Can you check if Miss Aliesha Mulholland has a cell comm on her with a functioning locator? Please press the position app on it,' says the voice, all deadpan like it really is a machine. It rolls its photo-fit eyes around until they fasten on poor old Aliesha.

'OK,' I say. But I ain't hopeful. Aliesha ain't got her bag with her and wherever she's left it I don't really want to go back looking for it. Instead I pat her pockets, which is easy because like me, she didn't wear Own Clothes. Maybe she ain't got any one pound to pay to Children in Need. Anyway, YOU OP Challenge Academy uniforms are like boiler suits. They've got one pocket over the breast and two at the sides and that's all, and God help you if you've got a comm in any of them.

I shake my head. I think about whether I'm going to have to go back down the service shaft and try and retrieve her comm from wherever it is. I start to panic. I'll have to try, because they've got to get us out.

'Please don't worry,' says the voice, and suddenly I notice it's changed its control mechs. It's gone into soft, deep, reassuring tone, very strong and very male. *My God, they think I'm going to go to pieces and do something that'll endanger all the others*, I think.

'I'm OK,' I say, trying to reassure my personal negotiator that I got myself well under control and everything.

'We need you to be very brave,' says the voice, hitting the lowest base control mech I've ever heard. 'We need you to secure the safety of Miss Mulholland and move to a location where we can evacuate you. Once we have evacuated you, we can sit down with you to track back your movements so as to locate Miss Mulholland.'

'OK,' I say, my heart pumping ever so slightly slower.

The word evacuation is so sweet.

'Please activate your tracker app.'

Thank God the tracker app works. Once I'm out and they download it on to their grid, they can track every movement to comm made against a time plan and find Aliesha. 'Yes, I done it,' I say breathlessly.

'Well done, Leah,' says the voice, as creamy smooth as hot chocolate filled with marshmallow. 'You are a very brave girl.'

'What about the others?' I say. I think of Connor, always of Connor, but all the other kids are down there in the gym too. I think of Ruby. I want to ask about her, but before I can say anything the chocolate voice says, 'Please listen carefully, Leah. We are only going to repeat the location you must get to once. The longer we spend on the comm, the more the probability of hacker viruses overhearing. We wish to get you out immediately. Can you make a rendezvous in thirty minutes?'

I know I can get to any place in the building in that time, even with crawling back down the vent system, but it depends, don't it. Depends on the Eternals.

'OK,' I say. A new feeling tugs at my stomach, a feeling like I'm rolling downhill all out of control, and if I don't get this right I'm going to roll right off a cliff. And there ain't going to be nobody there at the bottom to catch me.

'If you can retrieve a comm with a working GPS, activate it and type in the code 1234. Can you remember that?'

'Yes,' I whisper. Aliesha groans. I take hold of her hand. I press it gently.

'Before I give you the final evacuation coordinates, can you tell us, Leah, how many shooters there are?'

'About three,' I say. I know there's more, but what if Connor's one? I only saw three.

'And where are they holding the school?'

'In the gym,' I whisper.

'Do the shooters have control of Lock Down?'

'Yes,' I say, 'and they have grenades. Maybe.'

'Grenades? How did you collect this information? Have you seen evidence of this?' The tone in his voice has gone all flat, like now I'm exaggerating. Like I need to exaggerate.

'I just overheard it,' I say, wishing I could withdraw that, hoping it won't change my evacuation plan.

'OK, Leah.' The smooth delicious voice is back. I heave a sigh of relief. 'In your opinion are they actively shooting students in the gym as we speak?'

'No,' I whisper. 'But they shot some kids this morning. When are you going to get them all out?'

'It may take an hour or more for the team to assemble.

Regular patrol officers have secured the perimeter of the school and it's being kept under surveillance. We're briefing the SWAT team on the situation and have already set up a command post nearby. Are you following me, Leah?'

I nod, then remember my imaging app don't work. I wonder if he's going to talk a whole lot more before he tells me where to go. My battery icon has turned red. It could run out any minute.

'Leah? Do you understand?'

'Yes,' I whisper.

'We need information so that we can run background checks on any suspects. We need to fully survey the layout of the area and identify any known weapons involved, the number and disposition of the hostages, any potential motives, any information could be useful. Can you supply us with any information, Leah?'

Sounds like they want to compile a bleeding encyclopaedia. There ain't time for this. Kids are dying. What if my battery runs out? I'm suddenly scared it will. My palms start sweating.

'Do you know the names of any of the shooters?'

I hesitate. If I tell all about Markel and Lucas and Jase, they are *so* Damian's gang that the police are going to work out Connor is one of them too. They're going to target them all when they get in. Connor will get shot. 'Markel Mcleod,' I say. He shot those kids at point-blank range. I have to say Markel. 'And, I think, Damian, but I ain't seen him. But maybe not him,' I add. 'Maybe not his gang.' I feel an idiot. That must have been so see-through.

'Do you have any idea why they might be doing this? Any angle that we can start negotiations on?'

I want to scream *HURRY UP. GET ME OUT. MY BATTERY'S DYING.* But instead I whisper, 'Because.' I hesitate. I don't know why they're doing it. 'I think they're bored,' I say. It's true. I think that's why they're doing it. 'I think they think it's fun,' I add. 'I think they want to show everyone they can do what they like. I don't know.'

'OK, Leah,' he says, super chocolately, like I obviously don't know nothing and am just another thicko who goes to a YOU OP dump. 'Please go to the top corridor, third storey, M wing. Locate the big, picture, ground-to-ceiling window. The only window without a Lock Down roller grille. We are going to remove a section of the window and evacuate you. We are going to try to do this without compromising our operation. We will complete your removal at 13.15 hours. You have thirty minutes.'

# 12.45 p.m.
## Friday, 18 September

'But,' I start to say. It's not that I don't know the place. I do. It's the big window that looks out over Bradsmith Park. The posh park we don't have passes to. 'But . . .'

'Please be at the allocated location point in exactly thirty minutes,' repeats the voice, a little harder now; some of the soft base tones all gone. 'At 13.15 precisely. We cannot help you unless you can do this. We must cease transmission now.'

The phone cuts. I want to say about Ruby. But it's too late. I want to say that with my tracker on, I'll get to the cupboard and leave her water and then her location will be recorded too, but it might take time to do that, I don't know.

But he's gone anyway. I sit there huddled up for a minute. I try thinking about it. I know I got to go by Ruby and let her know, make sure they can get her out. I'm going to have to hurry. Got to get to the big picture window. I wonder why it don't have a Lock Down roller

108

grille on it. Then I remember it looks out over the park. That park got a Lock Down system all of its own. The residents of Bradsmith Park wouldn't like to see no windows covered in sheet metal. They was the ones who insisted on a picture window that'd look pretty and all. Thank God for the residents of Bradsmith Park.

I turn to Aliesha. I say, 'Ali, this is the water.' I gently tease open the fingers of her poor bloodied hand. I slip my fingers free. I flick up the nozzle on the water bottle and, holding her poor head very gently, I get her to sip a few drops. I hold my breath while I do it and squint up my eyes. It's funny but I don't mind looking at her face no more. It's kind of crusting over. She's probably going to lose the one eye. When I'm done, I press the water bottle into her empty hand. I close her fingers around it.

'Be OK, Ali,' I whisper. 'I'm going for help, then we'll get you out. We'll get you to a hospital. They can do good stuff now, reconstruct everything and all – we'll get you sponsored. Don't worry 'bout a thing.' I bleeding well hope we can get her sponsored. Since the last round of cuts, health care ain't free no more. But she'll be bound to get a sponsor after all this, won't she? Course she will.

Then I call Mum.

Like usual she don't answer. The call goes to voice message. Why the hell don't she bleeding well answer?

She too ill for that? And here I am calling her, like I'm not in a bad way? I just want to hear her voice for one last time. But I don't, and I don't have time to call back neither, so I leave a message. 'Mum,' I say, 'it's Leah. I'm just calling to tell you that if you hear about the trouble going on in YOU OP 78 it's OK, because I'm all right. I'm pretty sure Connor's all right too, so don't worry about it. I love you, Mum, bye.' And I snap off the comm.

I hope Connor *is* all right. I check my messages again to see if he's answered.

Nothing.

I wriggle over Aliesha and start my way back down the shaft. I'm thinking fast. Get down. Check. Stop. Listen. Make sure the Eternals ain't around. See if you can get Aliesha's comm. Keep to the labs. Get back down B corridor. Get back to Ruby. There ain't no way I can do that unless I use the corridors again. The corridors have all got CCTV.

*Oh, Anton, shut down the CCTV, can't you?*

But I'm thinking, maybe he can't. If he could have, he'd have done it. I exhale in a rush, trying to balance the hope and the fear, and think it through. I can get back up into the ceiling and try to get to her that way, but that'll be slow and I got to get to the picture window in time.

Nervously I lift off the tile to the lab den. I listen. I

stick my head out and it's like I got the extra-sensory things going on, like my ears are grown well big, and I can hear everything as far away as China. Except I can't, and I wouldn't want to hear nothing from China anyway. Since the People's Revolution Round Two started there, it's all gone nuts. We're told about it every day. How what happens to places when the people can't dig deep and take the cuts and think they are entitled to their human rights and all that.

But I listen like I'm listening to those army tanks in China anyway.

It's all quiet. No windows rattling, no distant popping, but I'm not fooled. They know I'm around, so I sit there on my heels and I try to figure out what I'd do if I was them, and knew I was around. I'd stake the place out. I'd put boys on every corridor and I'd bloody well get me – if I was them. But there ain't nothing. No footfalls, no squeaky give-away noises. In fact, it's gone so bleeding quiet, it's freaky. I check my watch. Twelve minutes have passed since I spoke to my negotiator. I'm in good time. I wish to hell I could just sprint down the corridors and get back to the library that way.

I drop lightly to the floor, the balls of my feet cushioning my fall. I roll back on to my heels again and squat down in the same position I was just in, only now

I'm three metres lower down. Still nothing.

Cautiously I shift forward and that's when my bloody comm starts vibrating again.

It could be Connor.

Desperately, recklessly, I snatch it out. But it ain't Connor, it's a number I don't know. Wasting the last of my battery. Should I take the call? What if it's one of the Eternals? But I'm going to take it. I make myself breathe naturally. It won't matter if it's them. They already know I'm around somewhere. My locator don't work anyway. All in a rush I'm suddenly really glad my locator don't work. I breathe out almost normally.

I'm going to take the call, because what if it's my Crime Reduction Negotiator on another line telling me of a change in the evacuation plan?

I take the call.

But it ain't neither of them. It's a voice I don't know. It don't use any fancy apps to get through neither. It's a straightforward voice call with a regular number. Instantly I'm ready to cut the call, but there's something in the voice that tells me not to, so I balance there, listening with my ears still reaching as far as China, listening to that controlled voice I'm hearing on the comm, as it says, 'If you want to stay alive, don't hang up.'

There's a silence. All I can hear is someone breathing.

I nearly hang up. I say, 'I ain't hung up.'

'OK,' says the voice. It's female and young. One of those educated posh kind of voices that is doing 'Slumming It'.

'So talk,' I say, because I ain't got time to do the polite chatting and breathing thing. If this voice don't know it yet – it better get to know it right away.

Suddenly the voice goes all hurried and urgent. 'My name is Victoria Jenson and I'm a reporter. Don't hang up. I got your number from Mrs Strickland, who told me you are a survivor hiding in YOU OP 78. Please don't hang up. I was doing parent interviews with Mrs Strickland. I'm over at your mother's; I'm interviewing her now. She's OK. She's doing fine, but I'm going to call the authorities to send over a welfare worker to stay with her.'

I breathe a sigh of relief. I hadn't realised how worried I was about Mum.

'Leah,' says Victoria, 'apart from you, every other caller reporting this incident at YOU OP 78 is being held in the gym. There's been no reports for a long time though. One of the last callers said their phone comms were being taken off them.'

'What's happening there?' I say. I can't help it. I need to know if Connor's OK.

'All the staff and the students are being held in the

gym,' repeats Victoria. 'You are the only one still free in the school as far as we know.'

I don't correct her for some reason. I don't tell her about Anton or no one else.

'Leah,' she says again, 'they are relaying images from cell comms from the gym. It's not good, Leah.'

'What's going on?' I say.

'Leah, believe me, it's not good.'

I want to scream then, but obviously I can't. I got to go. I got to get to Ruby. I got to check she's doing fine and I got to make my rendezvous, for frick's sake. I don't have time for all this.

'Leah,' says Victoria again, 'there's something not right and I want to warn you about it.'

'What?' I say. And I'm not impressed. Like does she think I don't know something ain't right? Plus reporters will say anything to get an angle, so I feel to hang up on her straight off.

'Leah, I've replayed the feed of images and I'm worried.' Something in her voice stops me.

Frick! *She's* worried.

'I got to go,' I say. I don't have time to do reporting. 'Call me later when I'm out. I'll sell you an interview,' I say.

'Out?' she says.

I don't have time.

'I'm going,' I say. 'Thanks for sorting out Mum. I'm gone now.'

'Leah,' she says again, 'call me back on this number. I'll stay with your mum till a care worker takes over. I'll protect her from the media as best I can. I'd really like to get your full story.'

I hang up. The press. She can self-appoint herself to anywhere she likes, and I can't do nothing about that. She don't really care about my mum, though. She just wants the scoop on all this blood, but if she looks after Mum, that's good for me, whatever her motives. Who cares what her motives are. Everyone's got motives. Everyone's got to do stuff to help themselves. That's how it is. That's the deal.

I got a motive too.

Get out.

Help *my*self.

# 12.57 p.m.
## Friday, 18 September

I slide into position beside the tech den door. I listen. Everything is still eerily quiet. I can hear my own heart hammering like doomsday in my chest. It feels like the whole world is going to hear it. If they're staking out the corridors, they must've got someone a bit cleverer than old Jase on it, because Jase is so ADHD he'd have given himself away a zillion times by now. I peer out into the lab. It's empty. I can't see Aliesha's bag neither. Well, there's nothing for it, I need to go – so I move. I'd rather have been rescued *after* they stormed the gym, I think, kind of vaguely. Why couldn't I have just waited in the vents with Aliesha until it was all over? I suppose my personal negotiator must've analysed the risks. I try to analyse them. I realise I'm expecting this to be all over pretty soon. But what if it ain't? And then I see the sense of getting me out. Like what if it goes on for hours? For days even? How would I manage then? I'd have to come down to use the loo anyway. And I laugh at

116

myself, like needing to use the toilet might be the death of me.

But what did that reporter mean 'something's wrong'?

Everything's wrong.

Everything's totally wrong.

Quickly I cross through the lab, through the next tech den. Everywhere is still as quiet as the grave. If I come out of the last lab and dart across the corridor into the computer rooms the CCTV will only catch me for a quick few seconds. Maybe they'll miss me, because by the time the sensor for the lights flash on and all that, I'll just have been a shadow, won't I? I try to convince myself.

Is it worth the risk?

I get to the door. I take a deep breath. I run. The lights flash on. Immediately sirens start. Christ! They've rigged the corridors. Rigged the light sensors. Rigged something. I'm so scared I slip. I feel my knee hit something sharp – a piece of glass. I'm on all fours and I haven't even made it to the computer rooms. I look down the corridor; it's glinting madly with specks of reflected light. The whole floor is covered in bleeding glass!

They've booby-trapped the corridor.

They knew I was in there.

They knew I'd have to come out.

They've scattered glass shards everywhere.

My knee is bleeding. The palms of my hands are sliced open. I pull myself to my feet, leaving a smear of blood along the floor. I get into the computer room. I won't be able to get to the ceiling again. I'll leave a trail behind me, a trail of blood smears. I'll never get out. I run through the computer room. The computer sensors blink and flash on. I don't know where I'm going now. I hear them. They're whooping. They're on my trail.

I hurdle over benches and blast past the Smart Servers area. I don't care any more about the CCTV on the corridors. They know where I am, so what's the point? I smash through the swing doors out of the computer room on to the short corridor that leads to the stairwell. Just let me get down to the library. It's like a replay from this morning. Here I am again. Slowly – at least it feels slow to me – I take in the learning I've made. Already I can mentally figure out how far to the lockers, how far to the toilets and how quickly the kids behind me have got to move.

Maybe I got a minute. Not a minute, maybe ten seconds. Enough time to lay a false trail? I'm thinking as I'm taking the stairs, four at a time. I hold out my poor sliced hands. I squeeze them up. I let the blood drop. When I get to the bottom, back to Level One, I hold out my hands again. The blood sprays from me, and as it's spraying I dart to my left towards the art block.

118

That's five seconds.

I check to make sure the blood's giving my direction away. Then I shove my hands up into my armpits and I clamp down on them. I skip sideways. I double back. I slip down along the walls, where the CCTV won't catch me, and duck behind the lockers.

I crouch. I hide. I wait. Behind me is the alcove to the toilets. My heart's rocketing in my throat till I think I'm going to faint.

The kid following me makes it down the stairs. There's only one of them. He's a lot slower than I was. I guess he ain't got the rest of his future hanging on his speed. In fact, he's not even trying to race. He's a plump kid who I only know by sight. He's carrying an AK-47. He peers at the floor, peers at the blood spray. I pray to God he's as stupid as the rest. He sees the pattern of the spray turning left towards the art block. He lets out a whoop and heads off that way.

I breathe in a rush of air. I feel dizzy. I'm trembling. My legs're shaking. My heart's shaking. For a brief second I let my eyes close. I can feel a strange prickling at the back of them. I open them up in alarm. For a minute there I thought I was going to cry.

For some reason I feel my way into the alcove. I know I got to go, got to get to Ruby, got to get to the big picture window. But I'm suddenly tired and I don't trust myself. I don't never cry. Last time I cried – apart from in the ceiling this morning – was when Mum decided she was feeling well enough to do the garden. We ain't really got a garden, just a strip of dust down the side passageway. She decided she was going to plant strawberries, because us kids never ate nothing nice like that. She dug it and all and bought these two strawberry plants and shoved them in the strip. That night I cried and cried. I don't fricking know why I cried like that, neither.

That slow kid's going to realise he's made a mistake pretty soon and turn back and hunt me down. The lesson-change music goes. Christ, lesson-change. The lesson-change timer must be set on automatic. But even as it goes a whole new opportunity opens up. The toilet doors behind me unlock. The toilets unlock! That is like a gift from heaven. Instantly I duck inside. The toilets are unlocked. I can't believe it. All I got to do is hide and wait for five minutes until the toilets go back on Lock Down. Five minutes and then I'm safe! The Lock Down system on the toilets is different from the exits. The toilet doors can be opened by students from inside the toilets only. That way kids don't get locked inside them, but nobody can truant into them during lessons. At the end of every lesson-change the teachers on duty do a toilet sweep.

If I can hide inside for five minutes, I'm safe. I pray God that slow kid won't figure I've gone into the toilet. But I have and I do. I go into a cubicle and I stand on the toilet basin and leave the cubicle door just a little bit ajar, so if that kid decides to check, he'll just glance though and see no locked doors and no feet on the floor and then he'll go away. I pray. I hope. He has to. He's probably not going to feel comfortable in girls' toilets.

He don't come back. I hear the lesson-change music start to fade out. The music lasts exactly five minutes and I know that bleeding tune by heart. When it starts heading for the last percussion bit you know you've only one minute left to get to class. It's the end of lesson-change. I'm safe.

I step down off the toilet seat and run my poor hands under the cold tap until the sliced flesh is cool and white. Each lip of each cut is curling slightly open. I take a wedge of toilet roll and bind my hands up and press them together until the bleeding stops. I bend forward and lean my head against the mirror that ain't really a mirror, but it's this panel of stainless steel that gives your reflection back anyway. My breath forms a slight mist on it. I know then I really want to cry.

I suck in my cheek and chew on my lip. I check my knee. It's only a bit cut up. It's got a scab of dark crusty blood over it already. I leave it alone. I flex my leg a bit to make sure the scab ain't going to bust open and betray me. It holds pretty good. Then I check the rubbish bin. I'm looking for empty water bottles. I find two. I swill them out and fill them up and thrust them deep into my pockets. Ruby's thirsty. I guess she's scared too, so I think of what else I can take her, but there ain't nothing else. I try not to go all weak again when I remember she asked for chocolate.

What am I going to do? I know one thing I'm not going to do – and that's give Ruby away. She's been lying there all quiet, too petrified to squeak, so I don't need to lead that boy straight to her. I got to get to her without nobody seeing. There is only one way to do that. It'll be slow, but I'll just have to bear it and go as fast as I can.

I'm going to take to the ceilings. It's going to be easy to get into them from here, because I can climb up on the loo seat and haul myself up on to the top of these flimsy partition walls between the cubicles. From there, if I can balance straight, I can easy reach the ceilings. So I'm going up. I'm on the right level and I'm going to crawl in a straight line back into the library space. I know I can do it because I know there ain't any walls in the ceiling, not in this section anyway. It's just one open mesh of ceiling struts and cable wiring and ventilation pipes and the Level B decking supports. Just a criss-cross of steel girders. I can duck through them and if I can stand up straightish, I might even be able to walk some places, from strut to strut, and get there quicker. I get up a bit of hopefulness and I thank God for Lock Down inside toilets and cool running water.

Inside the ceilings I can stand up. Not everywhere and not on the polystyrene tiles, but I can balance on the web of struts if I stick to the middle of each section. The decking overhead is high enough to allow me to stand upright. The only thing is, I'm not sure if it's going to be any faster. The aluminium web that holds the tiles ain't very strong. I'm pretty small and light, but they still creak when I step on them, unless I do it really slowly and just inch my weight forward.

So that's how I start. Inching my weight from strut to strut, taking my time and shining my comm on each bar before I tightrope-walk myself on to it.

But I'm getting there. Step by step I'm getting there. And the web of aluminium struts help me. They're like some bleeding huge chess set. I can go three squares forward and two sideways. I can plot out where I'm going. It's all maths. Each strut is half a metre square, nearly. I can estimate the distances. I can guess when I get to the corridor in front of the toilets.

Over the corridor I slow down. I move v-e-r-y

carefully. When I'm really sure I must be finished going over it, I squat down with my legs straddling a tile. I inch it up and check.

And I'm right.

I straighten up. I keep going. I get to the library. I check again. I'm just over the librarian's desk. And then I realise I can get to Ruby – right to her – without even coming down from the ceiling. I can move a tile over the book cupboard and check on her that way. I let out my breath and smile – just a bit – because now there's no way that slow kid has followed me. No way. She's safe.

I'm there. I lift the tile. I whisper, 'Rube it's me,' so she won't be scared.

And then I wait. For a moment I'm the one who's scared. I'm scared stupid she'll be dead. My throat dries up in a weird way.

'Leah?' she says at last.

And I feel even luckier than a winner of a Five Minutes of Fame and Fortune ticket!

'Rube,' I say. 'I can't stay. I've brought you water. They're going to get me out. I'm tracking your location on my comm. They're going to come in and get you out too, but I got to get out first, because they need your location from my comm – to rescue you.' I say it all in a great big rush, because it all sounds like bullshit to me, and that I'm just getting myself out and leaving her behind. Suddenly I can't bear myself. If I could I'd jump down into the book cupboard and swap places with her straight. But I can't. I can't even jump down into the book cupboard, because if I did, I wouldn't be able to get back up into the ceiling again, probably. Well, maybe I could, if the bookcases held. But I ain't got time anyway. So I just crouch there wondering where to drop the bottle of water, where it ain't going to hit her, or make her jump, or cry out.

'Leah?' she says again, like she just wants to know I'm there and that's all. Like she don't give a monkey's about nothing else and getting rescued is too far away through dark hours of waiting for her.

'I got to leave you,' I say, because it's true. If I stay nobody's going to come and rescue neither of us and Aliesha neither. 'So don't worry, yeah? I'm going to drop this bottle of water right where you can reach it. You just sip on it, yeah?'

It's going to have to do. I feel mean, because I'd planned on keeping the other bottle of water for me, but I'm going to get rescued in under half an hour, then I can sip juice and soda and anything I want, maybe, but it might be ages before they get to Ruby. And it's kind of my fault and Anton's fault that she's lying here wounded. I promised to help her, so I say: 'I'm going to drop the first bottle near you and the second one too. That's two bottles, yeah?'

'OK,' says Ruby. Her voice is so weak, so lost, so sad. I'm too scared to ask her how she is, if she's in pain, or if she's bleeding, or where the bullets hit her, because I can't do anything for her anyway. I can't even get down out of the ceiling to pet her a little and all that. I just don't have time. So I just drop the bottles of water next to her tiny curled-up shape. I'm really careful.

'I'm going to turn my comm off now,' I say. 'It's going to be dark, but I got to save the battery.'

'OK,' she says. I turn it off and it's horribly dark down there in that book cupboard. 'Bye then,' I say.

I've really got to go. I'm worried I'm going to miss the rendezvous. That voice didn't sound like the timing of the manoeuvre was flexible. If I'm late, they ain't going to wait. I'll miss that slot. They might need me to go to the other end of the fricking building before they'll find the right place to cut in to try again.

'Bye,' I say again, like I'm waiting for her to let me go. But she don't say nothing, so I straighten up and balance myself. I put the ceiling tile back. I inch myself away from the place and straighten up and start thinking about the huge picture window at the end of M wing.

There's just one last thing before I can get going.

Anton.

126

# 1.09 p.m.
## Friday, 18 September

I can't go without trying to take Anton with me. Deal or no deal. So I crouch on the struts and, like a Cossack dancer, I cross back into the library. 'Anton,' I hiss.

I can positively hear him smiling through the gloom. 'Thank God you made it,' he says.

'Even better,' I say, 'they're getting us out. Come on.'

Anton hesitates. He raises himself to a crouch as if he's going to come. Then he sinks back. 'Are we going to have to get down?' he asks.

'Yep,' I say, 'but we'll make it.'

'I can't take the CCTV out,' he says. 'They've put some kind of firewall around it.'

'Thanks for the intercom, anyway,' I say.

'Yeah,' he says.

'So you coming?'

'I can't take Lock Down out either,' he says.

'I know,' I say. 'The police told me neither can they.'

'But I can jam transmissions,' he says, 'if that's useful.'

127

I can't see how jamming up the airwaves is going to be useful. It'll probably make things much worse, but I nod anyway and say, 'Right.

'Anton,' I say, 'they're getting us out. Let's go already.'

He don't move.

'We've only got about ten minutes to make it,' I say. I check the time on my comm. Nine minutes actually.

'To where?' he says.

'M wing picture window.'

'But there's someone down there after you, isn't there?' says Anton.

Like that slow kid is going to stop me. 'Yeah,' I say. 'Look, are you coming or not?' I ain't got a lot of time to hang around.

'Sorry,' he says. 'I think it's less risky to stay put.'

I guessed as much. I had to try.

'They'll end this thing soon.'

He's going to wait it out, survive his way. That's the deal. But I got to survive too, and I need to go.

'OK,' I say. I turn.

'Make sure you make it, Lee,' he says.

'So you'd like to keep me alive,' I say.

'Yes,' he says quite simply, and inside that 'Yes' is a whole future of us hanging out together, of sharing an ice cream as it melts on a sunny afternoon, of trying to learn how to play chess, so he can beat me, of walking home in the misty autumn evenings, hand in hand.

'Catch you later,' I say and I'm gone.

The first half of the distance is easy, but it's long. It's stepping from strut to strut by the light of my comm. Only four minutes left. I'm hurrying. If I can get to the picture window at exactly the right time, then it don't matter if that slow kid comes after me. He'll just see me get away. That thought is like honey, thick and sticky and very, very sweet. Just for a few moments I allow myself to think about it: think about not feeling scared any more; how my racing heart will slack off. It means fresh air on my face, a glimpse of sky – and not through thick, blast-proof, popping, rattling glass, neither. I just can't imagine what it means. Then I take a dip. It means leaving Ruby and Aliesha. It means leaving Anton. It means leaving Connor.

Suddenly I'm feeling so guilty. I never even tried to find Connor. I never even tried to get him out. I just believed the worst about him. What kind of a sister is that? I'm supposed to take care of him. He's my little brother. He belongs to me. I've been taking care of him for ever. Why have I stopped now? I feel so guilty. I know he wouldn't be bothered about me. He wouldn't feel guilty. But I'm not him. I'm the oldest. I'm supposed to watch out for him, even when he don't want me to. For a split second I wonder if I can even leave him, but I know I'm going to. I really am. I ain't really got no choice, that's what I tell myself.

Maybe Anton's right after all. Maybe it's stupid to pretend Number One don't come first.

I get to the place where I think B corridor runs east–west through the building, from O wing to M. I try to follow it, as far as I dare. The light from my comm's going yellow and either my eyes are dying or the comm ain't going to make it. The icon is flashing red like it's got its own heartbeat going. If I'm not careful, I won't be able to call up nobody. If they change the evacuation point, they won't be able to hologram me in, nor nothing.

I prepare myself. I got to drop back down on to B corridor. And then I got to run – *make it to the picture window – please God let me make it*. If they see me on CCTV, they're going to come after me. I flex my leg in the gloom. I can run. I squat in the darkness above the corridor. I check the time. Two minutes. I measure it against the distance and the speed I got to go. I'm impressed with myself and my maths. I never thought I was good at maths, but it looks like I might be. Who knows, maybe one day I might even beat Anton at his stupid chess game.

I pull a tile up. I take a deep breath. It's now or never.

I drop down. There's no glass; that's good. The CCTV will pick me up. I got one minute and twenty-five seconds to make it to the picture window. Right now the SWAT team are probably cutting through the glass. They're probably going to come in themselves after they've got me out.

If I arrive at exactly the right time, I'm going to be able to just run straight out the window and straight into the hovercraft waiting for me. I start sprinting. I breathe like I'm an athlete. In and out on a count. I count. It helps. The alarms rip into action. I don't care. Then the alarms stop. There's Anton's jingle. No more alarms. *God bless you, Anton.*

That was clever of them to substitute the intercom for the alarms though. I mustn't underestimate them. I wonder if that slow plump boy will get the job of getting me again. I still don't care. I can outrun that kid. He can't shoot straight. I'm going to get to the window and jump clean through it before he's even figured out where the trigger is.

I'm running. I'm gliding. I'm soaring. I'm thinking of ice cream. I'm going to eat one massive vanilla-cherry tub with chocolate and sprinkles. I'm going to kick the seeds off dandelion heads and punch out the sunbeams that filter through the old trees on my street. The sweet wrappers in the gutters are going to sparkle like gems; everything's going to be sparkling like gems. I'm going to pick up old Sal from school early and not care and I'm going to hug her up and maybe even go to Young Carers' X Factor and let her come too.

The footsteps behind aren't catching up, no way. I'm the rocket man. Up ahead I see the big picture window. The B corridor stretches straight past it. There it is up ahead, on my left. It's funny but I can't see no glass being cut. Never mind, they'll have some different super technology. Probably technology that evaporates glass. Poof. Gone. But as I get closer, I can't see nothing happening around that window. I check my watch. I'm dead on time. Even a bit early, like by thirty seconds early. Maybe that's it.

I'm too early.

After all that worrying about being late. And slow boy is behind me. I know it.

Here's the window. My chest is dry, hurting. I can't breathe no more. Where the frick are they? *There's no SWAT team here.* Maybe they changed the evac. point? *Make it to the next set of lockers.* The SWAT team are going

132

to be coming through that window soon. Slow boy will have to turn and run himself back where he came from. I smile at that thought, at how the tables are going to be turned. Then I hear popping. That kid is shooting at me and that is so not going to happen.

I duck behind the lockers. The kid stops. He's seen where I've gone. He's laughing and he's wheezing and he's shouting, 'I got you now, sucker.' But he's doubled up trying to catch his breath. He's waving the gun around. He's standing right in front of the picture window. Right where the CCTV can't see him. And he's got his back to the window. He's silhouetted by the sky. *He's standing right in my way*. He's so plump he looks almost girly.

And it's exactly 13.15.

And a precision-strike missile, no bigger than a Coca-Cola bottle, smashes through the picture window and silently blows him away.

# 1.15 p.m.
## Friday, 18 September

I make to run to the window, like I'm still going to be rescued, because I can't think of anything else to do. I'm still stuck on that idea, on that vanilla-cherry ice cream. How I'm going to hear how Ruby gets rescued and they can rebuild Aliesha's face and I'm going to learn chess and Connor wasn't one of them and everything's going to be all right.

But it's not.

I can't get used to it. There's no window any more. There's not much of the corridor left, just a shelf, and what's left of the plump kid is lying on it. A mess. There's a gap the size of a grapefruit in his head, right where his face was. He ain't got no back of his head left, neither. He ain't got a body he's attached to, just one arm flung out in a surprised way down the corridor. If you didn't know it was him, it could be anyone. It's just a mess. I back right away from him. A mess of meat and blood and glass and corridor. And that's all. I turn away. My stomach

134

rises into my chest and my mouth turns acid. I struggle not to be sick. I back right away from him.

But where's the SWAT team?

'*I'm here,*' I croak. '*I'm here.*'

But there's no sign of nothing.

I stop. I back up to the lockers and hide. I'm still expecting someone to come swinging through the window and all. Swing me out. I reach for my comm. It's gone dead. The batteries are well and truly off. Just when I need to hear from my personal negotiator. I'm scared. Maybe that plump slow boy wasn't alone.

And still no one has swung through the window.

I don't know what to think. How long should I wait? What should I do now? I got to wait. Maybe they was delayed. I got to hide. I crawl into a locker and shut the door on myself and crouch down, all crouched up small. I just stay there hugging my knees and everything.

That could have been me waiting there by the window. I can't get the thought out of my head. That could have been me. They must've shot that boy to save me. And I think how clever they was – that they even knew he was out there chasing me. They must be *really* clever and have special surveillance. They must be so clever they know everything. They're so clever they'll think up a new way to get me out. They knew they couldn't do it then because that boy was following me. They know I'm waiting here. They're probably trying to call me right now. Why did my comm have to die right when they're trying to call me?

But if they're so bleeding clever why ain't they here and getting me out? That's what they should be doing. I want to scream, 'THAT'S WHAT YOU SHOULD BE DOING.'

But they're not. And I'm waiting and waiting for them. It's well gone 13.30. Must be, and that's not precision timing, is it? They could so easily get me out now. I don't know why they ain't doing it. I peep through the crack in the locker door to see if they're coming, but nobody's moving out there. And then I know they ain't coming. And I could have been dead and I'm going to be dead if I get caught now.

And slowly I realise *I am dead*.

*My private negotiator must have thought the figure by the window was me.* I've been killed by some accident when I should've been rescued. And now I ain't going to be rescued no more. And I crouch there in the darkness of the locker, getting used to that feeling – of not being rescued – and of being dead – and of freak accidents that kill you when they're supposed to save you.

Something's wrong with it all. I can't work it out. This

136

ain't how it's supposed to be. Me crouched up in this tin locker. Dead.

And freak accidents.

And then I think maybe it *wasn't* a freak accident? But what kind of accident could it be? I think, how can a missile nearly the size of a Coca-Cola bottle be an 'accident'? If they didn't know it was that plump boy and they thought it was me, how can that be an accident?

And my brain don't work properly.

Because I know it can't be no fricking kind of accident. It ain't no stupid accident. But if it ain't no accident, then it was meant. It was done on purpose. And that's the bit I can't get my brain round. That missile was a precision-targeted super-strike something or other, bound to be, like what the SWAT teams get to use when they take out their enemy targets in films. Neat. Precise. Silent. Minimum damage.

And if it was on purpose – then that missile was 'meant' for me.

And I am an enemy target.

Then I got to stay and crouch up some more, just trying to get used to that idea. And I can't. How can you get used to the idea that the people you called up to get you out are trying to kill you?

And why me?

Why am I an enemy target? Something's wrong here. What did I ever do, except get late for school this morning?

This morning? I try to go over it again. Maybe it was something I did this morning.


*This morning?*

*Connor slams the door behind him. He leaves.*

*Sally looks at me, her bottom lip trembling.*

*I say, 'Wait here.'*

*I run upstairs. I wear my school uniform, boiler suit, jacket. It don't matter no more. I ain't got a pound coin anyway. Own Clothes Day ain't about looking good, is it? It's about collecting charity, ain't it? Like I believe that.*

*I run a comb through my dark hair. I do a side parting. I flop a long fringe over one eye. I put on a scarf and drape it around my neck, like a gunslinger from the Wild West. I look OK, even pretty. Then I belt back downstairs.*

*'C'mon,' I say.*

*'Leah,' Sally says.*

*'S'OK,' I say.*

*'Leah,' she says again, like she's got so much to say, she can't even decide where to start, and it's all beyond her.*

*'Look, ol' Sals,' I say. 'It's not your fault. OK? Leah's in a bad mood. OK? Even if Leah's in a bad mood, she'll still take*

*care of you, right?'*

*Sal nods.*

*'School, shall we?'*

*She nods again. 'Sing?' she says.*

*My turn to nod. 'You choose.'*

*Sally sucks a finger in delight.*

*I'm forgiven for shouting.*

*I grab her backpack. I'm going to be late. I'm going to have to walk her all the way to Daisy Bank Primary. Even if I run all the way back to the bus stop, I'll never make it. And that means a detention after school and that means being late to pick her up from Latchkey Club, and that means no X Factor. I take her hand and start singing. I know my bottom lip ain't trembling.*

*At least not on the outside.*


No. I never did anything wrong.

I did my best. If my best wasn't good enough, it ain't my fault. What was I supposed to do? Was I supposed to fricking search Connor's bag? Was I supposed to know what he was planning? Do they think I'm in with him? Was he even planning?

I shift uncomfortably in the locker. And I think about that. How I stopped trying to read the signs about him long since. Even after the early riots when he came home with that stupid 3D TV and said his friend gave it him. Sally was happy. She likes TV. She loved watching it in 3D. I didn't do nothing about that. Nothing. Nothing. Nothing. I sat and watched the thing and I knew it wasn't no present from nobody. I knew something was wrong. Maybe I *am* in with him. Maybe saying nothing, not reading the signs, means you're guilty as hell.

Maybe I deserve to be an enemy target.

But a precision-strike missile?

I don't understand it. I can't understand. And my battery is dead. I can't even bleeding call them up to get them to explain why they just tried to kill me. But I can't crouch in this locker for ever neither. It's too bleeding small for a start. And at least I should be grateful that no more Eternal Knights have showed up to finish me off. I peep out through the locker door again just to be sure. Why haven't they showed up? Even if they were too far away to hear the strike, they must've seen it on CCTV? But how can you finish someone off if they're dead anyway? Something's very wrong.

'Something's wrong.' Who just said that? Someone said that just this morning.

And that's when I see that dead boy's comm.

Just centimetres from where I am.

Thrown from his hand when he fell, it must've skidded

140

right to my feet. It's like a sign, one little hopeful sign in all this mess.

I reach out of the locker. Those boys will turn up soon. I hesitate, scared to move. The comm lies there. Its battery icon is green and full. I pick it up. It slips beneath my touch. It's all bloody. Thick lumps of blood cling to it. I never knew blood could lump up like that into such thick, sickening, liver-ish clots. It's a good job I ain't eaten since last night. My stomach heaves anyway, raw, dry, empty convulsions.

I pull the comm inside the locker anyway. I wipe it off. I cradle it against my chest and think about calling up my personal negotiator to ask how come he tried to kill me instead of rescuing me, because I still don't get it.

And the comm is still on. Someone is still talking. I lift it from its cradled position in my lap and hold it to my ear.

'Come in, Brandon,' says the voice.

'Brandon?' says another voice.

This comm must have multiple-way receivers. I open the locker door a little and check the receiver channels and it has. I'm about to turn them off so I can use it, but then the voice says:

'We saw the window crashing on CCTV. Have you eliminated Leah Jackson?'

141

And it's Damian.

My mouth sags open.

Brandon must be the plump kid.

'Brandon?'

Before I can think about it, I whisper, 'Copied.'

'Brandon?'

I pull my scarf over my mouth and slam the locker door. The sounds muffle everything. 'Yeah,' I say. 'She's dead.'

And Damian says right back, 'Excellent.'

I grunt.

'What was all the fireworks?' says Damian.

'Window broke,' I grunt.

'You stay on patrol,' says Damian.

I grunt again and make like I'm wheezing.

'Cover B level.'

I'm listening. I don't know what to think, what to say. But I don't say nothing because I'm dead and suddenly that feels like a relief. I think I'm going to stay dead.

I'm sure I'm going to stay dead after I hear the next thing.

'All other Eternals on Leah Jackson duty. Mission over. Return to base.'

And then I know I *am* going to stay dead. That is majorly weird: accepting I'm dead. I know it's just a fiction, but somewhere inside that story lies my real

142

death. If I don't play this out really carefully, I really am going to turn that story into a fact.

And that chills me so much I start shivering.

And I'm shivering and shivering, thinking if I'm dead then no one's looking for me and if I'm dead then I can weirdly stay alive.

Anyway, nobody comes to check on nothing. And I don't know what to do except stay dead. If someone came to check, they'd see I wasn't dead and Brandon was. What am I going to do about that?

So I think about it. I think and think, but I don't have a solution, except that there's a mess in the corridor, but it's not me. If I can do something, maybe I can keep the fiction going a bit longer.

But I don't know what to do, except leave some of my stuff around the body and hide stuff that'll show it's Brandon. So take off my scarf and throw it on to the corridor floor. I come out the locker after a bit. I slip along the side walls and I pick up any bits of Brandon's stuff that I can. There's only one shoe, because the other is blown away. I stuff Brandon's one shoe in a locker. With one foot I drag my scarf through blood and stuff. I throw my comm on the floor. I hope that will fool them. I look for his gun. If I could find his gun I could defend myself. I could creep up on the Eternals, creep through the ceilings and shoot them. Dead.

POW. POW. POW.

Could I really do that?

I mean: would I miss? I also mean: could I kill someone?

If it was to save everyone?

If it was Connor?

And there *is* his gun. It's on the far side of the demolished floor. I pick my way past Brandon, past what was Brandon, the gluey mess of bone and brain. There's a huge blob of grey semolina-like stuff right in the middle of the far side corridor. I can't bear to look at it.

I slide down the walls. I keep my eyes on the floor. I ain't going to look at that grey, blobby, lumpy thing. I'm going for the gun. I edge out from the wall as far as I dare. There it is. There's the gun. It's right there. A bit too far to just get easily. If I stretch out an arm, the CCTV will see it. But you can't tell from an arm if it's me, can you?

Maybe you can. How much do I want the gun?

I want it all right. I want everything it stands for. And I want it now. I stretch out my arm. I get hold of the barrel. I drag it towards me. It slides on the floor with a rasping sound. And I pick it up.

Now *I* got a gun.

And it changes everything.

# 1.55 p.m.
## Friday, 18 September

I got a gun. I crouch back inside the locker, cradling it. I got a gun. I think about leaving. I think about using the gun. I think about how I'm a hundred per cent safer now. It's nice and heavy. Not too heavy, but like it's solid. I weigh it in my hand. It feels good. I run my finger along the matt barrel. It's beautiful. This gun is the most beautiful thing I've ever held.

I think about calling the police again. But I don't. Having a gun won't protect me from them. Will having a gun make me a target for the SWAT team, though? I'm a target already, aren't I? Probably. At least I was. Wasn't I? I still don't know how I came to be a target. I'm dead now. It's less risky to stay dead. Anton is definitely right. You've got to take the less risky options in life. And in death too, it looks like. You've got to take care of Number One.

I should leave. I can't stay here. I can't think where to go. If only they could turn off Lock Down.

145

*Lock Down . . .*

*Of course, I made it into school late.*

*But at least before Lock Down.*

*Lock Down.*

*Lock Down, the new government solution to everything, from rampage to lateness. It's so simple: Lock Them Out.*

*Whether they're rioting or have missed the bus.*

*The idea is that it gives you a wake-up call. You know: Oh, I am so locked out of school, shall I press on the alert buzzer, so that I can drag an assistant head to the video link screen who can then tap in a code to the remote while I hang my head? Oh, goody, then I can be escorted into Internal Exclusion for the first lesson and be lectured about Personal Responsibility, and Failing to Plan is Planning to Fail, and It All Starts With Me, and statistics on how Tardiness is a FACTOR in FAILURE, and how I'm destined to be a LOSER by the time I'm eighteen (if not before – considering my family background – and my mum – not said – but in their eyes – and – oh – they like the American twang 'Tardiness' gives to their new policy), and, oh yes, I obviously WON'T be going on to higher education.*

*Lock Down.*

*Another brilliant brainwave on how to turn a LOSER into an A\* WINNER.*

*Shall I press that buzzer then?*

*Or shall I straggle off down the town and sip Coke in the café by the station and hang out with all the other losers?*

*And plan a riot.*

*Lock Down.*


If only I could turn off Lock Down.

If only I could create enough carbon dioxide. If only I could flick the switch on the high-voltage field. If only I could get out the picture window. If only it wasn't three storeys up.

Where can I go?

If I go back to Anton, he ain't going to help me. Am I really going to creep through the ceilings and shoot Damian? I need to get away from here. There's this smell now, and I might be sick. I can't get back up into the ceiling from here. I need to get back to a girls' bathroom; that's where I felt the safest.

I wait. I hide in my locker. I just wait until the pips go for the end of lunch break. When they start the music, I come out of my locker. I go sliding back down the sides of the corridor until I get to the first girls' bathroom. I go in. I get into a cubicle. I stand on the toilet and leave the door half open, but my heart ain't banging so hard any more, because I know they ain't looking for me. The music stops. The pips go for the end of lunch. The door locks down. I know I'm safer than I've ever been. I'm more lost than I've ever been. And I want to talk to someone. I want to talk to Mum.

So I call her.

I'm careful though. I'm using Brandon's comm. I turn off the multiple-wave banding, and the GPS locator and the tracking device. I shut down the hologram facility. I shut down the Bluetooth Web access. I just reduce it to what my crappy comm could do before it died. Before I died. I hide the outgoing identity number and voice identification app. I put it on mech voice so I could be anyone.

Or no one.

I call Mum.

'Hello?' says a voice. It's not Mum.

'Who's this?' I say, ready to flush the comm down the toilet before it gives me away.

'It's Victoria.'

'Victoria?' I struggle with my memory, trying to dredge up that name and then I get it, the reporter this morning, the one who said she was personally going to stay with Mum to sort her out. The reporter who offered me the scoop. I remember something. It was her who said, 'Something's not right.'

So staying with Mum sure has its uses, including Mum's comm.

It's like she can read my thoughts. 'My name is Victoria Jenson. I am filtering calls for Mrs Jackson. Everyone's been calling.'

'OK,' I say. 'Is Mum there?' I twist my lip up into a strange shape and bite down on it. Tears start into my eyes. And I can't say nothing else. I just want to hear Mum's voice. I don't care if she's down or nothing. I just want to hear her.

'Leah?' says Victoria.

I just gave myself away, didn't I? I think about saying 'No,' but I don't. I swallow. I try to speak. I have to breathe in. Wait till I got control back. 'Please don't tell no one,' I squeak at last.

'She's taken a sedative. She's a bit out of it.'

'Don't tell anyone I'm alive. I think someone just tried to kill me.' I'm back on survival mode. I ain't going to hear anything from Mum. What could she have said anyway? It don't matter no more.

There's a moment's pause.

'Not them,' I say. 'Not the kids. Someone from outside, some kind of mistake.'

'What happened?'

I tell her. I don't know why I do, but I got to tell her.

149

I don't cry or nothing. It all just comes out like I'm checking up on a shopping list. Someone just tried to kill me, not Damian and his morons, someone from outside.

'Leah? I want you to listen very carefully,' she says when I'm done.

'Yeah?'

'Leah? I've got a very bad feeling about all this.'

Like *she's* got a bad feeling. She should try being shot at, having precision-target missiles launched at her sometime. But I *am* listening.

'They're not going in.'

'What?'

'The SWAT team are not going in to end the siege.'

I try to get my head around that.

'They say they want to try to negotiate a clear outcome before they storm in.'

I gulp. It's not good. Not for me, nor Anton. Nor Ruby, nor Aliesha bleeding all alone.

'But in siege situations that's not policy,' says Victoria.

'No?'

'Leah, it's usual to do R.A.I.D. – Rapid And Immediate Deployment, with T.N.T. – Tactical Neutralization Teams, using A.S.D. – Active Shooter Doctrine – that's straight in and shoot to kill all hostage-takers, because of the potential loss of life. In other words, they risk a dozen deaths to save hundreds. C.C.N. – Control, Contain and Negotiate – only takes place where there are hostage situations below critical mass, maybe just one or two hostages, where any death is a casualty.'

'Oh,' I say, trying to figure all that out.

'It's not what you think, Leah, that matters. It's just not policy and that's what makes it weird.'

*C.C.N. – Control, Contain and Negotiate.*

They're not coming in. They're not going to rescue us. Why the hell aren't they? Why the hell are they going to Control, Contain and Negotiate? The picture window and the missile, that wasn't Control, Contain and Negotiate, was it?

'Now *you're* telling *me* they've used Active Shooter Doctrine on an *evacuation* mission. That's not credible. That sort of thing doesn't happen. I hate to say this, but have you considered they might have lured you to that point precisely to kill you?'

'What?'

'Would you know why they might want to do that?'

What's she saying? I'm reeling. I ain't got a clue. This reporter lady's telling me they ain't coming in. I'm not going to be rescued. I've been had like an idiot.

'Have you considered that the siege might be very convenient for the government?'

'Convenient?'

'Given the new police powers they want to press through parliament, given the enormous debt crisis, the huge rise in population and the ongoing recession?'

I still don't get it.

'Leah, think. If they close YOU OP Challenge Academies and send third-tier students straight to Volunteer Programmes, think of the savings.'

'Close YOU OP Academies?'

'No more running costs, no more teachers' pensions, no more compensation suits, huge savings.'

'But they can't do that; they've got to educate us. People won't buy it.'

'Unless the nation sees third-tier students as a threat.'

Sees third-tier kids as a threat? I think of Anton and Ruby and Aliesha. We ain't a threat.

'If there was a clear choice between wasting public funds trying to educate dangerous, anti-social, feral children – who with each class they go to, get more savvy on how to undermine our society –'

*Dangerous, anti-social, feral children* – the old clichés. But it ain't right. Surely people will know it's just a few morons. How can a few morons spoil everything?

'If there was a clear choice between that and putting

those same children into positive For The Greater Good programmes –'

I can see where this is going.

'Programmes which would give these same children a role, teach them a trade, instil in them the discipline necessary to reduce their delinquent behaviour, what do you think people would go for?'

'But,' I say, 'that's not right.'

'Only because third-tier students haven't used up all their credibility yet.'

'I don't get it,' I say.

'After YOU OP 78, they will have no credibility left.'

And the penny drops. If Challenge Academies hothouse school shooters, then Challenge Academies will be shut.

'And there's the news feed.'

And that will be the end of going to school, and that's it.

'They're relaying images from inside the gym directly to the news channels.'

'What news feed?' I say. Without warning I'm all agitated. What're they showing? Is Connor there? Has she seen him? Has Mum seen him?

'Nobody's seen your brother,' she says, mind-reading me.

And suddenly I love this stupid old Challenge

Academy. I love its stupid corridors and its stupid rules. This is *my* school. They can't close it down. Miss Carter wasn't *that* bad. She was strict and all, but you've got to be strict with some kids or they spoil classes for the rest. And anyway, she didn't deserve that bullet. Nobody deserves a bullet through their brain. Challenge Academies ain't that bad. They're quite good even. If you do well and get through your Five Minutes of Fame and Fortune you can still go to college. Anton's wrong. There is a future. It's not a fair one, it's not an easy one, but there still is one. If you work hard and all.

'Not that that means anything,' she says. 'All students' identities have been digitally amended.'

'What's going on?' I say, suddenly the tone of her voice sobering me.

'It's not good, Leah. They're killing the kids. They've set up an Internet forum and are getting the public to vote on who to kill. Like it's a reality TV show.'

'*What?*'

'Who to kill,' she repeats.

'No,' I say. I shake my head. I don't believe it. Jase and them set up an Internet forum? You've got to be kidding.

'Yes, Leah,' she says. 'They're calling it: "*Have Your Slay Time*".'

I freeze. Here in this building? My stomach rises. It

sticks in my throat and it ain't a nice feeling.

'Leah?' says Victoria, 'there's something wrong with it all, and even more so because Active Shooting teams aren't going in. If the Eternal Knights, this shooter gang, are really doing that, the police shouldn't be negotiating.'

I clamp my mouth shut. I try not to think about it. It's impossible to think about it. And I don't believe it. Shooting kids is one thing, but making a game out of it?

'Leah? I want you to do something.'

'What?' I whisper, my voice quite hollow.

'The outside world needs to know the truth about what's going on.'

I nod.

'Leah, you're the only one who can help all those parents.'

'Me?'

'Leah, they need to know how bad it is.'

I shake my head.

'If they know, they can bring pressure on the police to go in.'

I really need the police to come in.

'We need to understand why the government are holding back, what their stake really is. We need to expose them.'

I just need to get out.

'Leah, I want you to find out what's going on.'

*Find out what's going on?*

'Negotiating could take hours, days even – that's if they even start negotiating. We've heard nothing about that yet. If this gang are doing this *Big Brother*-style vote-in "*Slay Time*" – lives are going to be lost.'

Days! I can't wait days! I got to get out. Ruby needs medical help, Aliesha's got to get out. Anton's waiting. What does she mean?

'What do you want me to do?' I hear myself saying.

'I want you to film what's going on. If you can. Can you?'

I gulp. I breathe in. The washroom smells of stale urine and bleach. I think of the gun lying on the wash stand. I think of looking down its sights at Damian. Could I? Even if I could get back into the ceilings (which I could), and even if I could tightrope my way over to the gym (which, now I come to think of it, the way the ceiling is all laid out, I probably could too), but even if I could do all that, I don't want to film kids getting shot. Maybe this Victoria wants to put kids getting 'slayed' on her own channel. Maybe she's a sicko. I've seen enough people getting shot. I saw Miss Stupid Carter getting shot, right in front of me. I saw Brandon get blown up, I saw those kids in the library get it in the forehead. POW. POW. POW. I can't see no more. It ain't good for me.

But *could* I do it? That's the question. Could I do it to end all the shooting? You know: *could I shoot them?* Shoot Damian, shoot the Eternal Knights? Shoot Connor?

For the greater good?

'Leah?'

'Yeah,' I say wearily.

'I need to know. The public need to know. We'll pay you.'

I want to laugh then. She'll pay me? And that'll make it OK? You can buy anything, you know. But I don't laugh. Instead I say, 'How much?' I don't say: like will you still pay if I don't make it?

She'll *pay* me. That is such a joke.

'This is an entirely private deal. We will not reveal you as our source. This is all being said in the strictest confidence. We'll pay enough so your mum doesn't have to worry any more.'

Ouch. She's hit me where I hurt. Mum needs cash so badly. If she had money she could get better health care. She wouldn't get so down. She could care for Connor more; send him to a fricking shrink; Sals could go to a better school, not have to end up at another dumpster Challenge Academy like YOU OP 78.

*Not have to go to any Greater Good Volunteer Programme, neither*.

That clinches it for me. I don't ever want my Sally squatting on a toilet seat, being fictionally dead and wondering when she really will be. I don't want Sal doing five years of unpaid work neither, just because she's from a third-tier family.

'Half upfront, right now, deposited in my mum's account; email me evidence,' I say. 'I can check the email from here. Then I'll go. I'll do it.'

If I can.

If I can put a bullet smack between Damian's eyes. I'll even film that for her.

But suddenly, just as I've decided I'll creep over the ceilings and take Damian and his crew out – be my own little SWAT team, just me and my old gun. Use A.S.D., Active Shooter Doctrine, all on my little own, right to the max – I suddenly think: But *should* I? *Should I do it?* Is it OK to kill even if it is to save others?

'Great,' says Victoria. 'I'm authorising payment right as we speak. We can go higher according to the coverage you get us. Use your comm. Relay live images through your video channel via band 78. I've set it up specially. 78. Remember, like YOU OP 78. Now, if you want to check out what's coming through already on G.M.B.,

158

General Mobile Broadband, just tune in; you can see what's going on in the gym on N.N., on National News. You can see N.N. has posted the websites that are hosting this new "game" show. Link in to *Have Your Slay Time*. It's all there. But I want live footage, with that real-life, real-time edginess, and I want it relayed straight to me.'

She is a sicko, ain't she? A sicko who talks in stupid jargon.

'OK,' I say. I don't feel good about this.

'Oh and Leah?'

'Yeah?'

'Don't call the authorities.'

Like I was going to call Commander Bloody Peterson ever again. But all I say is 'Why not?' I don't wait for an answer though. I'm already paranoid someone's going to be hacking into my connection and locating me. Already afraid another precision-hit missile is going to come searing through the wall to take me out. So I say, 'Don't worry, I won't.'

'And Leah?'

'Yeah?'

'Get footage of the guns they're using. I want to try and source who's supplied all the firepower.'

'OK,' I say. 'But you've got to do something for me.

You've got to get everyone to put pressure on the police to get us out,' I say. 'They say Lock Down can't be disengaged remotely. They told me they can't do that. But they can. They must be able to do something. The whole exterior is still humming. That means the electricity's turned up to max. The high-voltage field is buzzing like *Lord of the Flies*. I can hear it right through the walls, right now. Get them to do something.'

'All I can,' she replies.

I hang up. I look at my weapon. I take some footage of it lying there so innocently on the wash basin. I don't send it to Victoria. When I get out she can have her gun pictures.

At a price.

*If* I get out.

# 2.20 p.m.
## Friday, 18 September

I pace the floor of the girls' toilets. I look at myself in the mirrors. Thin, dark eyes, round like coins, anxious. My reflection scares me. I open the news channel on the comm. Victoria's right, they're hosting a show called *Have Your Slay Time*. I flick it on. There it is, the inside of the gym. Our gym. I can see the trampolines standing at the end, the painted brickwork of the interior, the Olympic-turf flooring, the basketball courts marked out in royal blue. I can see the benches in tiers and the kids sitting on them.

It's our gym all right. There are the Eternal Knights. They've got masks on. They look like Zorro the Greek in cargo pants. They're holding guns. They look like the guns I saw Markel and Jase use in the library. I try to see if you can read the make or model numbers on the guns, but you can't. I scan the masked faces, searching and searching behind the masks to see if any of them are Connor, but the camera roll switches. It's panning away

161

from them. You can't really tell who they are, anyway. The camera's zooming in on a bunch of scared-looking Year Sevens. I search their faces. I don't remember none of them, neither. A roll of script is running below the picture. It reads 'HOST CHANNEL FOR *HAVE YOUR SLAY* HAS DIGITALLY ALTERED FACE RECOG'.

I want to laugh at that. They're digitally altering the way the kids look and that's going to make hosting a vote-to-kill show OK?

The camera carries on zooming in on the row of kids at the front, on the first bleacher. I notice they are all tied up. They're sitting in a little line, like they're convicts. I watch as one of the Eternal Knights walks up the row placing black hoods over their heads. When he's completed that, he faces the camera with a grin and says, 'Welcome To Death Row.' The news even rolls those words in large black caps across the screen. '*HAVE YOUR SLAY TIME* WELCOMES YOU TO DEATH ROW.'

I don't know why I'm watching this.

It's insane.

One of the Eternals drags a kid to the front of the gym like it's an arena. He faces the camera and says, 'You get to vote if he lives or dies.' 'VOTE ON SIEGE YOU OP 78,' roll the screen words. And then he does it again with the next kid, but this time he adds, 'Don't forget, one of them

162

must die. Who will it be? It's your choice. Vote now. If we don't get nuff votes we're going to kill them both.'

It's horrible. It's too horrible to believe. I don't believe it. I don't want to see which kid gets killed. I flick to another channel. There's a group of parents talking about their kids still inside the school. There's a helicopter hovering over the playground. There's a headmaster from Challenge Academy YOU OP 77 saying that 'Lock Down was never intended to be abused in this way'; and 'short of extreme force', which might 'spook the killers and ignite a bloodbath', there is 'simply no override to the system' and even if 'the power grid is shut down', the 'school's internal supplementary source generators will simply take over'.

I flip off the viewer. I lean against the wall. I remember Victoria's words. 'Can you find out what's going on?' Can I? If that's what's going on, all I want to do is retch.

And put a bullet through Damian's skull. Just like that. POW.

And Markel's. POW.

And Lucas's. POW.

Jase too.

POW. POW. POW.

And Connor?

I start a text. *Priority*. **Try to hack into the live feed** from the gym that's going 2 the news. Try to break it or at least jam the transmission. L

I look for Anton's number. Stupid. Anton's number ain't going to be on this comm. And that's all. Wearily I hoist myself into the ceiling. I set my mind to the purpose. I can't fool myself. I am going to have to kill five kids, maybe more – unless they throw their weapons down. Maybe Connor is not one of them. I hope to God Connor ain't one of them. If he's one of them I'm not sure I can kill him.

And I realise I ain't doing this for Victoria, nor for the money. I'm not really doing this to save the others. *I'm not even doing it for me*, for Number One. That'd make Anton laugh, wouldn't it? This is all about Connor.

I sigh. Imagine that. Connor. I'm climbing into the ceilings, toting an AK-47, steadying my mind to kill kids, and it's all about Connor. Yeah, him.

You see, I've just got to know. I got to know if he's past saving. I've been trying to save that kid for so long I can't stop now. So I got to know.

A part of me flickers away, seems to laugh at myself from behind some closed door in my head; laugh and say: Even if he is past saving you won't be able to stop trying. And I know it's true. I ain't never going to get away from that kid. His hooks is so deep in me, even if I do get out of all this, if I don't know what's up with him, and I don't try to save him, I ain't never going to be free. Either way I'm still going to be under siege.

I got to know.

And that's all there is to it.

I'm dead already, anyway. I've been dead for a long time. Connor made sure of that. Connor made sure I never even got a life. Any kind of happy carefree life. All the lies, the blame, the threats, the thefts, the tempers, the refusal to help – the making-things-as-difficult-as-possible-for-everyone. And that's funny, because it looks like he was getting himself a secret life all along, getting to be an 'Eternal Knight'. How come I missed that? How come all of us missed it? When did it start?

Did it start?

In my heart of hearts I know he's one of them. I know that even if he ain't one of them, he'd *like* to be. I know. That would be so right up his street. I sigh. I must be passing above the dance studio now.

How come we just let him get like that? Did he search for himself in them silent times when all he done was grunt at us? Did he ask himself what kind of a person he was going to be, and find there was nothing out there for him, that he was already used up before he was even started?

Why didn't he fit in?

Was it because he was the only boy? Was it because all

the rest of us done things differently? Was it because we moved house so often he never got to know who he really was? Was it Mum's illness, Dad gone, or him? Just him. Just a fricking mental head-case. A no-name, no-person with no identity, not wanted by nobody?

He made sure of that. He never wanted to fit in. He never rated nothing we did. He made it difficult for everyone. He made a world that he couldn't fit into. And suddenly I'm mad at him, for being his non-self, for making every thought I ever get keep going straight back to him.

He played that part, didn't he? He chose it. He chose to drift to the bottom of everything. He didn't *have* to. He just chose it. He chose losers for friends. It was all him and his stupid loser attitude.

I trip on a strut and nearly fricking fall.

Maybe all them Eternal Knights all drifted to the bottom and made their own little loser gang so they could all be big shots and all the rest of us deserve to get it – because we've built a world that can't stand them.

All that throwing stuff and smashing stuff and telling us it was all our fault.

As I straighten up again, I nearly miss my footing too. I stop. Try to calm down, I tell myself. But I'm all upset now. I mean, how come I got to be like his *mother*? I'm *not* his mother. Why do I have to *feel* like his bleeding mother?

It's not fair. I sway on the struts between the poly tiles. I've lost my count. But I don't really need to be counting, because I'm beginning to hear a murmur of voices.

The gym.

It's near.

I freeze.

Here I am fixed above the world, one of the un-dead. And down there is where they all are: the Eternal Knights and all the dead to be.

And Connor.

And I don't know what to think except I really wish he was dead too. And I hate myself for thinking that. I hate myself for thinking and hoping he might die. If he died I could be free. And that's funny, because here I am in the ceilings, like I'm a new kind of species. Ceiling life. All I got to do is pick my way across the quilt of struts, duck under the girders, count the squares, do the maths, and find out a way to pop up a tile and take aim and POW, he's dead. But I ain't going to do that. I know that even if I take out Damian, Markel – all of them, I'm going to try and save him, even if I get it instead.

I ain't never going to be free. And that's all.

I step out again. Getting across the ceilings is suddenly so easy. How come all I ever did before was crawl? Stepping out on the struts is fast too. There are some parts where you can even see properly, where the difference between Level One and Two just goes sheer up to skylights. There's darker bits too, where the decking for the floors on Level Two means you have to duck and stoop and walk like you're always trying to do a limbo dance or something. And there's the spiders' webs, thin threads: delicate, fragile, all swaying and quiet, all trembling, like they're waiting for the end of the world.

I stop. I must be above the gym. I breathe slowly. Take your time. One false move. One creak and it could be your last. Stay focused. Be very sure you don't make no false moves.

I pause mid-stride, listening for anything that'll tell me exactly where I am, exactly how far I got to go to be directly above them. I don't hear nothing that tells me anything. But out there in the gloom ahead of me I see the additional girders. They run in diagonal distances up to the ceilings, to an apex a good four metres above me. They must be there to hold up something. I try and remember if the gym has got a second storey above it. Can't have anyway. Them beams are holding up a roof. A pitched roof with corrugated covering.

I pause. In that case why hasn't the government landed on it, and drilled through it to where I am? That way they could get in and do the job straight. I don't think the high-voltage fields go *over* the building too. The angle of the pitched roof ain't that steep. It's no Swiss chalet. They could do it easy. But I give up wondering. Maybe Victoria's right. But then maybe she ain't. Journalists are always dreaming up conspiracies. That's their job. They got to make the government look bad, so they get paid.

It's all about getting paid, ain't it? And here am I getting paid too. At least, I hope I am. Abruptly I stop and get up the comm. I check that I am. Yep, there it is: a whacking fifty grand. Maybe getting paid ain't all that bad after all. It'll sort out Mum and Sally. If Connor and me go down it won't be so awful; there'll be money.

I pause as the noise from below suddenly gets much louder. My heart starts hammering. I have to check the comm to make sure I really did turn the GPS off. I gather up courage. *You're* the *hunter* now, I tell myself, like I'm in some action adventure book. *You're the hunter now*.

I step out over the struts until I know exactly where I am. I'm under the apex of the roof. Right here must be the centre of the gym. Around me are a lot of cables and some sort of wired packing on the struts. Electricity, I think. I mentally make a note of them, so that when I turn off the light on the comm I don't touch none of them. I don't want to trip up and somersault straight down through the tiles, and land in a heap right in front of Damian and his stupid gang, do I?

Carefully I squat. Slowly I inch up the corner of a tile. You can't believe how slowly I do this, how much my hand trembles, how hard my blood pumps.

There they are: the Eternal Knights. But they ain't got no masks of Zorro over their faces now. There's Jase and Markel and there's a ginger-haired loser from Year Eight. I've never noticed him before. He's the kind of kid that makes zero impression on you. He's lining up menu cards from a takeaway pizza parlour. He's got four of them and he's trying to get Jase to tell him what kind of pizza he wants, but Jase says, 'All of them. All of them. All of the ones they do.' So this ginger-haired kid is yelling down his comm, 'Send us all the pizzas and we won't kill no one.'

And there's Damian. He's got himself a kind of king chair made out of workout mats. He's lounging on it on the stage that they use in assembly. It's a weird kind of king chair. Four of the Eternal Knights stand guard round him, like he's a sultan. Those four all got on some kind of uniform. In fact, now I look closer, they're all wearing some sort of paramilitary gear with black and grey camouflage pants and black T-shirts over that.

And then I see him.

Connor.

# 2.43 p.m.
## Friday, 18 September

Yes, it's Connor in a stupid black T over stupid camouflage black and grey trousers, holding a stupid gun. He's wearing a stupid belt packed with stupid ammunition across his puny caved-in chest. He's standing stupidly over a stupid king chair made of green rubber workout mats. And he looks stupid. He looks a whole lot more stupid than he usually does, because all the military stuff just underlines what a loser he is.

I stare at him, and I'm sighing like he's a kid who's entered for a swim show and is going to do a belly flop. So now I know and now everything changes again. Well, in my head it does. Before, if I could've wiped out all of them with one round of gunfire, I'd have done it. If Connor hadn't been one of them, I could have looked at them like they was the enemy, like they was all evil, anti-social lowlives and I could have gone POW. POW. POW. And liberated us all. But now I can't. I can't do it, because all I see is a bunch of little

171

losers who're all far too pathetic to kill.

And if I kill one of them, maybe I'm going to have to kill all of them. And I can't do that. I can't do nothing that'll end up getting Connor killed.

Not while they all look so pathetic.

And he is going to get killed, isn't he? Does he really think he's going to survive all this? Does he think that SWAT, or the army specials, or whoever sees fit to bust in, are going to say, 'OK, boys, game's up. Put down your weapons and come quietly'? I want to shout, 'This is not a stupid video game, Connor. You ain't going to get no second life, nor third, nor however many damn lives like you think.'

I put down the gun. I rock back on my heels. I cover my face. How can I shoot such stupid little losers? What the hell am I going to do now? I'm squatting, just rocking, just thinking. I don't get no clear thoughts neither. I just don't know what the hell to do.

I give up. I'll just do what I got to do then. I'll do what Victoria says. I slide the comm out of my boiler-suit pocket and check it's on silent before I switch it on. I'm tempted to flash her and double-check what exactly she wants, but I don't because that might mean talking or listening and any noise might give me away.

With my comm on mute, I tune into the National

172

News. There on the screen is the gym again and there's the row of kids with black bags over their heads, all sitting there ready to be dragged to the killing chair and have their fates decided for them. There's Damian shouting, 'He's got to go! Your votes say he's got to go!' At least, I suppose it's Damian. The black Zorro mask and the digital altering of his voice mean it could be anyone.

That *is* strange. His black Zorro mask? I peer back down through the crack in the ceiling. I'm right. *Damian ain't wearing no black Zorro mask.*

Maybe the newsfeed ain't live. Maybe they *was* wearing black Zorro masks, but they took them off. I lift up the gun. Just to see what it feels like. Death Row, huh? I point it at Damian. I get him fair and square on the digital gun screen, the little black cross right in the middle of his forehead. Maybe I could kill him. It'd be pretty easy to. Maybe I really will.

I look back at the comm screen. I flick to the website address that's scrolling across the bottom of the newsfeed page. I click in. There's a cartoon of a guillotine and there's a cartoon of a row of kids with black bags over their heads waiting. Above every head is a joke name like 'Jane Doe' or 'Roger Mortis' and a box with KILL NOW? yes or no and a dancing arrow saying PRESS PRESS PRESS.

And under each kid is a tally and a countdown.

I bite the inside of my cheek. He ain't so pathetic after all. I think I *am* going to kill him. I double-check. I flip the comm channel back to the news. I check it's on mute. And there's Damian again screaming his head off and the scroll banner saying: HE'S GOT TO GO! HE'S GOT TO GO! HE'S GOT TO GO! YOU VOTED FOR IT! Like the message is: Don't blame me, I'd have swapped him out for a decent pizza.

And I'm just about to squeeze that trigger and stop Damian's little game once and for all, when I notice something. A chill flickers down my spine. Victoria's right, there *is* something weird going on. I bite the inside of my cheek. Victoria's definitely right. Something *is very* wrong. Down there through the crack in the poly tile, through the square metres of air between me and them; down there below me in the gym in question – *there is no Death Row. There is no little line of hooded victims.*

*There is no killing chair.*

I try to get used to that. What the hell's going on? There's just a bunch of puny Year Nines in blackish, paramilitary, stupid costumes whining for pizza.

It's a moment or two before this sinks in. I flick back to the National News and *triple*-check. I peer down through the crack in the tile. It's true. Nothing they are showing on the news matches. I scratch my head. Two stories. Two fictions. Except one ain't fiction. I believe my eyes. Down there they ain't playing no Internet *Big Brother* with kids' lives.

And I don't get it.

I don't get it any more than I get that Coca-Cola-sized missile thing.

I prop the gun against my knee. I pull out the extendable headphones on the comm. I got to try and get it. Maybe if I turn the comm off mute and listen in I'll be able to figure it out. I push the ear pieces into my ears. I settle on my heels again. I watch the news. The kids are sitting in rows on the benches. They're all digitally altered. That might be to protect their identities like they say. I scan again just trying to match colours from the news to the real gym below me. Nothing matches up. It's our gym on the news though. I still don't get it. What does it mean? I bite my lip. If it's not our gym then this video must've been made earlier. And I don't get that.

*But I do get it.*

Victoria explained it. I just can't believe it. Everything what Victoria said is true. We are all being manipulated.

*How can they do that?*

How can you prepare a whole reel of breaking news? Not just a news flash, but hours of the stuff. How can you invite the entire globe to focus in on what's happening in our gym and invite them to vote: yes kill 'Johnny Corpse', let's watch him beg and scream, let's all watch him – when it's all a lie?

But ain't someone going to notice something's fishy?

I shake my head. I flick back to the website. People actually *are* voting in. People are actually voting in to kill Jane Doe. *Normal, regular people are voting in.* I can't believe that. I just can't. They really believe kids are being killed in the gym.

I look back at Damian. If there really had been kids sitting down there on the front benches with black bags over their heads, I'd have shot him. I'm sure I would. I swear I would. I ought to have. I ought to have saved them. I pick up the gun again, imagining it. Yes, I'd have done it. Holding a gun gives you a nice feeling, you know. It means you can do things, change things, save little kids with black hoods over their heads. Yeah, I'd have saved them. But there ain't any kids going to be shot. And killing someone is not as easy as you think. So I lower the gun again.

All that's down there is the staff, sitting tense and dejected on the back benches; Mr Olusegun looking like if he had his way he'd tan the lot of them, Mr Farnham looking sad like he was wishing he'd taken early retirement last July, and Miss Mason picking at the bits of fluff on her jumper. And there's the kids, shuffling, whispering, crying too. One girl in a pink tank top is bawling. I think she's even getting on the Deputy Head, Miss Turnbull's, nerves.

They ain't killing no one. *HAVE YOUR SLAY TIME* ain't happening. There is no DEATH ROW. But they *are* being held hostage. And some kids did get killed. I saw Markel kill some. I saw him kill Miss Carter. Maybe I should shoot Damian after all. Maybe I should shoot Markel too. Would that make me as bad as them? That's what the police would do, wouldn't they?

Suddenly, just as I'm trying to decide if I should or should not, the air is shattered. A loudspeaker booms out:

'THIS IS COMMANDER PETERSON, YOUR CRIME REDUCTION NEGOTIATOR. WE HAVE BEEN TRYING TO MAKE CONTACT. WE WOULD LIKE TO TALK TO DAMIAN PHILLIPS. WE ARE PREPARED TO NEGOTIATE. WE'VE SET UP A SECURE CHANNEL. JUST PRESS YOUR TALK BUTTON AND YOU WILL BE AUTOMATICALLY DIVERTED TO OUR CALL CENTRE.'

# 2.58 p.m.
## Friday, 18 September

It's like a sign from the universe. I should not kill them.
I should negotiate with them first. That's what the police
would do.

Damian picks up his comm. He's feeling so big, ain't
he? He looks out at the school, sitting there whimpering
on the benches. He looks at the other Eternal Knights,
bored, flicking the pizza flyers around. He shrugs, like:
What the hell, who cares, it's all the same to me.

I flip my comm setting to conference channel. I enable
the multi-wave banding function. I press my ear pieces in
more tightly. I'm going to listen. My heart thunders, my
stomach feels like I swallowed a bag of nails. Commander
Peterson. I don't know how to think about him. How do
you think about someone who tried to kill you? I mean a
*real* someone, not stupid Year Nine losers who could kill
you all the same. No, *a real someone* who you'd expect a
lot better from. And suddenly I'm not sure. Did he
actually, *really* try to kill me? Or was he just defending

178

me from Brandon? Should I try to call him again? Maybe I should. Maybe I should try again. I start listening.

Damian makes himself comfy on his workout mats. I nod my head slightly. I've seen the Lock Down remote. It's lying right beside him. Right there on the king chair. Right beside the assault rifle, the arsenal of other stuff, the handguns, there it is, the Lock Down remote.

'THIS IS COMMANDER PETERSON, YOUR CRIME REDUCTION NEGOTIATOR. JUST PRESS YOUR TALK BUTTON. WE WANT TO NEGOTIATE.'

Damian does his what-the-hell shrug again. He presses the talk button.

'Is this Damian Phillips?' says Peterson.

Damian don't say nothing.

'Am I talking to Damian?' repeats Peterson.

I notice the way he has gone from 'Damian Phillips' to 'Damian'.

'What can we do, Damian, to resolve this issue?' says Peterson – all pleasant, like 'this issue' is a playground fight.

'What you offering?' says Damian, sort of interested.

'Say what you need,' says Peterson.

'Ten million, Swiss bank account. Untraceable. Private helicopter to get us out. No Interpol.'

I wince. He's been watching too many movies if he

179

thinks getting himself out of this is going to be that simple.

'We can talk then,' purrs Peterson, and I get the feeling he's setting up the GPS on a Coca-Cola-sized missile right as he speaks. All he needs is the exact coordinates, down to an area of one square metre. He can take out Damian and not touch a soul.

'No we can't,' says Damian, like he knows that too. 'You do all that and hail us, then we'll see. Meanwhile I'm giving my comm to the head teach to hold.' He cuts the connection. Not as stupid as he looks then.

But now I'm wondering. Is that what this is about? Money? Will Peterson set up the deal? Do they really think they'll get out? Will they take hostages with them? What will happen to the rest of us? I look at the gun. Should I shoot him now?

I don't know what to do. If I shoot him, will Markel just take over? Will I have to shoot him too? And who will take over after that?

I'll wait. I can wait. Maybe Peterson can get us out. I wish he'd bleeding well hurry and get us out. I turn off the multi-wave banding function. I tune in to see what's going on, on the news.

It's National News. The camera pans round. I see a face. A military negotiator. Underneath runs the

BREAKING NEWS banner: BREAKING NEWS. FIRST
NEGOTIATIONS OPENED WITH HOSTAGE TAKERS.
The minute the military face speaks I recognise the voice:
Commander Peterson.

I stare at the screen. I think I'm trembling. I *am*
trembling. He looks so calm and friendly, just like his
warm, chocolatey voice. You'd have to be nuts to believe
he ain't got total control over the situation. He looks
clearly, sadly, encouragingly into the camera like he ain't
never seen anything as bad on his watch before.

I can't take my eyes off him. I can't. I really can't. I
keep going over that precision-hit strike, that bottle-
shaped missile which zapped through the picture window
and reduced Brandon to raspberry jelly.

And in that split instant I grow up. I see behind that
face. I see that you can smile and charm, that you can
convince and reassure, that you can be grown up and
powerful and have everything – because I bet he has
everything and a nicer house than ours and good food in
the fridge and everything – and you can be rotten inside.
Worse, you can live with yourself and do TV interviews
after negotiating with killers and annihilating sixteen-
year-olds.

And you know, I'm shocked. I'm more shocked by
that than by moron Jase with his stupid brain. Because

181

moronic Jase don't know what he's doing very much. He knows he's killing someone all right, but he don't know why, and he's just feeling mean and following orders, because nobody ever gave a sausage about him.

That's how I think of it anyway.

And then I look at Connor and I don't know what to feel no more, so I rock on my heels and don't feel nothing.

Commander Peterson's saying, 'I can't reveal details and of course I may need to terminate this interview at any second if a return call comes through . . . but be assured we've been trained to negotiate with hostage-takers and we have every reason to believe that we can strike up meaningful dialogue.'

I don't like the way he calls them 'hostage-takers', like they never blew Miss Carter's brains out. I'm interested in what he's going to say next, but someone interrupts. Some reporter shouts out, 'We haven't got *time* to negotiate, Commander. They're *already* on their infamous website looking to *murder* – to *publicly murder* – eleven-year-olds.'

'We have taken steps to close that website down,' purrs Commander Peterson.

'But it's gone viral,' screams the reporter. 'It's no *use*. It's *live* on every portal. Unless you close off the entire Internet, you *can't* stop it.'

Commander Peterson smiles briefly. His tired eyes tell of real hardship – real leadership – of loss of sleep even – which is weird, because this has only happened today. His eyelids seem to droop slightly, as if he knows the size of the problem he's up against – the terrible choices he alone has to make.

I flick the comm over. He's so phoney. I just hate that. I hate phoney people. I bet he did try to kill me. I bet he really did. He looks like he could do that and not bat an eyelid. Victoria wants shots of the real thing. OK, she's going to get them. I don't know what the effect will be, if it's going to help or not, but I'm going to film what's really going on. I'm going to blast this weird charade sky high.

Carefully I edge myself into a comfortable position, one that I can hold, one that I can film the majority of the gym from. I stare at the kids sitting there in little groups. I stare at the teachers with their hanging heads, trying not to meet anyone's eyes. I stare at the benches and the trampolines and ropes and the Olympic-turf. I stare at the kids.

Quite a lot of them are crying now. Maybe the negotiation announcement set them off. One girl is very upset. She's got her head tucked up so tightly into her arms you'd think she was trying to pull it off. All you can see is her pony tail and her shoulders heaving. Heck, they're really shaking. It kind of makes your heart cut. I think of Sally. I think of Ruby. I nearly spoil the whole bleeding thing by thinking of them. The kid looks up and wipes her nose. You know, I think I know that kid. It's Tilda, the one whose mum texted. She's alive at least. Her mum'll be glad to hear that. Quickly, stupidly probably, I send a text to Victoria. **Tell Mrs Strickland Tilda's alive an OK. But please don't let her text back cos I can't do nothing more for her.** I hope I ain't giving myself away. But she's a mum. I wish my mum would text. I send it anyway.

Right. Now the world is going to get the truth. I turn the camera on again, and start filming. It's easy. I pan round from stage to king chair to Eternal Knights and weeping students. I touch in the app to forward the live feed direct to Victoria's comm channel. That's what she wants, ain't it?

I wait there gently tilting the camera from one end of the gym to the other. I span the width, and zoom in on Damian, zoom in on two of his 'bodyguards', on the Deputy Head teacher, Mrs Turnbull. She's still in pain; I can read it in her face. I catch Miss Perkins whispering to Coach Tenby. I zoom in on a couple of the Year Tens I don't like much. I just zoom in on them for the hell of it. I don't zoom in on Connor though.

I set my comm down at an angle and prop it up, so it just carries on filming. I check the battery. It's full. These new fancy comms can recharge themselves even when there ain't no sunlight. Then while it's doing that, I open up another Internet window and flick back through the news channels. I touch in the channel number Victoria gave me, 78.

It's really weird. I'm watching the news and I *am* the news.

There it is, the gym beneath me, Damian and his stupid king chair. Him lounging on his pile of workout mats. It's worked! Victoria has relayed it straight through to the nation! Wow, that is so strange. Other channels will host it soon. I flick forward through the other channels. And I'm right. What I'm filming is coming through live from two or more stations. It's got BREAKING NEWS in a banner scroll under it. It's being rolled right out across the nation! The rolling title bar now reads: BREAKING NEWS – LIVE COVERAGE REAL TIME FOOTAGE OF THE HORROR – SHOW SCHOOL SIEGE.

It's so majorly weird. I tilt the camera and the news tilts. I zoom the camera and the news zooms. I flick back to National News. They ain't showing the row of hooded kids sitting in their pathetic little line no more. Surprise.

They got two talking heads going instead. That's weird too. Why aren't they showing my footage?

Anyway, they're interviewing some bearded man. Underneath scrolls his name. I can't quite read it. It says something like: Professor V Important Psychiatrist from Psychiatristville. And he's talking to Superior Psychologist and Sociologist, Mrs Knowitall.

I listen.

PROFESSOR V IMPORTANT: The culture of alienation, inherited chemical brain imbalance, allied to poor parenting, low intelligence and peer pressure may predispose towards violent rampage, but it's the fermenting of these elements in Challenge Schools that is the tipping factor . . .

MRS KNOWITALL: But surely not enough to turn children into killers? Isn't it rather the brewing pot of *entitlement* that attending Challenge Schools fosters in the young, which manifests in anger at society? In short – they are biting the hand that feeds?

PROFESSOR V IMPORTANT: Whilst we may disagree on causality, one thing is for sure. The further we look into the current educational programme we offer YOU OP children, the more the roots of social violence will become apparent.

That annoys me. They didn't ought to talk like that about my school. YOU OP Academies are OK. You could get morons like Damian anywhere. You could. I bet you could. Maybe Victoria ain't such a conspiracy theorist after all. Maybe they really do want to close down my school.

I think about that. I flick back to the commercial news channels. They're still showing my newsfeed. I continue filming. Nobody's editing or changing none of it. Why aren't they showing it on National News then? It's majorly weird. Although maybe not. National News is so pro-government.

From below me I see Damian reach for his comm.

I don't know what guides me, but I want to hear this call. I flick on to the apps screen. I touch in the multiple-wave banding function again. I pull out the extendable ear pieces. I plug myself in.

'What's going on?' barks this voice. It's a voice I've never heard before. 'I thought we agreed no cell comms on, no live footage, no newsfeeds in or out.'

Quickly, I scan across the benches, scan the kids, the teachers, and I realise there's not a cell comm out. That's odd. Damian must have taken their comms off them. What does the voice mean? There's no cells on. Nobody is looking at the news. Certainly not the Eternals anyway. As if they'd ever watch the news.

Nobody except me.

Damian looks perplexed. He stares into his comm. He flicks channels. He starts watching the live footage I'm filming.

'Cut the live feed,' says the voice, 'immediately.'

'There ain't no live feed,' says Damian.

He checks. The Eternals are playing with their comms all right, but only on computer games. You can see that straight off by the way they're hammering the control mechs.

Through the crack in the ceiling, I see Damian checking the news again with a puzzled face. And I know what he's seeing, he's seeing the film I'm taking of him checking his comm with a puzzled face – cos I'm filming him doing it right now.

And suddenly I know that was not such a good idea.

Damian looks up at the ceiling.

Shit. I try to swing the camera away. It pans out past the teachers' benches to the trampolines at the far end of the gym. In a flash I see all the kids' comms piled up in a ball basket. Nobody has seen the news. Nobody knows what they're showing on the national channels. Except me.

And Damian.

And he's worked it out. He's seen the angle of his face. He's seen the angle of the camera pan and he knows where the live feed is coming from. He looks straight up. Straight at me.

He sees the crack in the ceiling. He's looking straight into the camera. I go to grab the gun. He grabs his Mac-10.

For a moment time freezes. I try to straighten up. I try to get him in my sights. I try to rise. Not fast enough. Not fast enough. His Mac roars. I try to roll, try to dance out over the web of struts.

I'm not fast enough.

I'm blown backwards.

# 3.15 p.m.
## Friday, 18 September

The force of splintering aluminium catches me. The impact sends me shooting over tile and tile struts together. I hear polystyrene fracture and snap. In slow motion, I watch bullets pop through the ceiling all around me. Straight lines of fire, random blossomings. Damian's trying to guess from the cracking tiles the direction of my fall.

I roll. Somehow I'm rolling along a line of joists. My feet are trailing, dislodging tiles. I lift my leg. I've been hit. There's blood. I see blood in the broken light that rays up through the bullet holes. I see blood on the ruptured tiles.

I hit a beam, an old RSJ, a solid, metal, weight-bearing beam. I cling on to it. It stops me. I realise in a din of screaming from below, that if I lie along the beam the bullets can't get me. Bullets can't kill through four metres of solid steel. So I lie along the top of the beam. I twist my leg up and press down on the place that feels white hot, feels sticky. I search around for the gun, feeling with my open palm, trying to see the gleam of metal through bullet beams. It's gone. I don't know where. It's gone. Must have fallen. Spun away from me. I'm bleeding a lot. It's like white fire shooting up my leg. Don't let the blood give me away. I lie frozen. All around me the ceiling pops with gunfire. Rounds of ammunition empty into tiles. The whole place looks like a sieve.

It stops. It goes quiet.

Someone screams.

I should've fricking killed him when I had the chance.

They're thinking of a way to get up here. I'm so fricking scared. It ain't going to be long before one of them shins up a rope and sticks their heads up right next to me. I got to go. My leg. I got to get back along the struts. I got to get back to my locked toilet. My leg? I can't make it. My heart is hammering so fast. They don't even know I ain't dead. And now I am dead. I'm going to be dead. I'm bleeding. They're going to kill me. I should get the hell straight out, bleeding or not.

Except for one thing.

My nose is pressed up against something. I lie, blinking in the pinpricks of light, listening to the shouting. I can't see exactly what it is. It's square-ish, like a bale. It's light coloured, about the size of a kiddy's backpack. It's cool to the touch and on one side of it is a small digital screen. And then I see, stencilled across the widest part of the pale bit:

*Explosives: handle with care.*

I'm trembling. I can't hardly hold steady. And I don't know why suddenly I think of Anton. Maybe it's the way he selected the ceiling as his retreat, back in the library, back in that before time – before I died – as if he knew ceilings could hide surprises. But I do think of Anton. I stare at the off-white package. I stare at the little digital screen. It ain't ticking. There aren't even any numbers on it. It's just snugly resting up against the main joist of the ceiling.

'What's happening?' I hear a voice in my ear. I realise I still got the extendable ear pieces wedged in. The comm's still in my hand.

I touch the apps screen out. I stuff the comm down my front. I'm sweating. The RSJ beam is clammy against me. Those kids don't know there's a bomb up here. They can't know. If they'd put a bomb up here they wouldn't shoot into the ceilings like that. One bullet, that's all it'd take. One bullet and the whole place will blow.

I stare at the package. Has it got a timer? I can't see one. I daren't touch it. If it don't have a timer, it must be set up to detonate remotely. A chill runs through me as I work it out. Just like Lock Down, somebody out there has a finger on a user touchpad; somebody is hovering a cursor over a detonate click tab. Somebody can press down at any minute.

BOOM.

The gym will go, the kids will go, the staff will go, I'll go. My mind jumps to Anton again. Can he hack into it, isolate it, do something? But if Damian and the Eternals don't know about it, then who? Who set it? Someone must have. Packages of explosives don't set themselves. I stare at it. It ain't got no dust on it.

It's been set very recently.

Must have.

I roll aside right to the edge of the beam, as far away from it as I can. I need to get out. I need to get away from it. How far do I need to get? Will it blow up the library too? I need to tell Anton. I pull my comm back out. I write a message.

**Bomb in gym ceiling sending footage – can you hack into it? Stop it? Library may not be safe you have to move.**

Stupid. I can't send the message. It ain't my comm. I try to remember Anton's number. *I can't remember*. I never noted it. It was always just there to click on. *I need to tell him*. I could send the footage to Victoria? That might make it worse. They might just blow us all up. I'm going mental. I can't think straight. *I got to tell Anton*. I'm going to have to move.

I pull up my leg to examine it. It's still bleeding. It ain't broken. I sit up and wriggle out of my boiler-suit top. I pull my T from inside, up over my head and off. I put my arms into the boiler again, dress back up. I start on the leg. My T-shirt was torn anyway so I don't care. I tear it some more, until it's a bit longer and can do like a bandage. Those kids are planning something. They'll be up here any minute. I knot it round my knee and bind the wound up tight. I flex my ankle. I try standing. I rest the wounded leg like a police horse does, standing at the end of the street, swishing at flies.

They'll be swarming up into this place. I'm right. Already I can hear them pulling out the climbing ropes, yelling at something. I pull myself up, force myself to stand. It's hard to balance. I must get back over the struts. Escaping ain't going to be easy. I'm kind of woozy. I stagger. The roof above me swirls. I'm on a boat, a boat pitching from side to side. I'm down on all fours. I can't track straight across the ceiling. I'll have to crawl. There's no ceiling left. It swims beneath me, ripples, ebbs. I got to stick to the edges.

I wonder about blood loss and shock. Is that what's

happening? But there's no point in wondering. If I can't balance and skip back over the struts, I'll crawl. So I crawl. Like a baby, I lower my arms and feel for the beam and drag myself forward. I go like that along the beam, one hand then the next. I reach the edge of the gym ceiling right by the wall. I haul myself down beside the brick gable. I find a niche left empty for some reason. I heave myself into it. I curl down. Just need to rest. Need to rest and catch my breath.

Four of the Eternals burst up from the gym below. Up they come over the edge of the gym wall straight into the ceiling. They bust through the tiles. Dust swirls. Polystyrene floats out like it's snowing. Four of them soldier through the dust and gloom and snow. They don't care if they make a noise or a mess or nothing. The half-light streams through. I can't see properly.

'Can you get them?' shouts Damian.

One of the kids pulls a gun and sprays bullets. Hailstones of bullets, snowstorms of white polystyrene.

'Who's up there?' yells Damian.

My teeth are clamped so hard, I've forgotten about my tongue. One of the bullets is going to rip into the explosives. We're all going to go BOOM. The kids stop firing. Gradually my jaw slackens. I realise I've bitten into the flesh all along the side of my cheek.

'Can you see them?' yells Damian.

'Nuffin,' shouts one of the Eternals.

I pull my legs into the alcove tighter and tighter. I stop breathing. I close my eyes. Why the hell did I come here? I don't know what I'm doing any more. Why am I doing anything? I should have shot the hell out of all of them.

The kids start weaving their way across the struts towards the gable. If they round the projecting bit, they're going to see me. I start biting down on my nails, gnawing at the hard flexy stuff until it rips in peelings. A bit snags on the quick of my finger, but I don't stop. I rip it out. Somehow the pain helps. What am I going to do?

I'm suddenly terribly, achingly hungry. It's like the bleeding has wiped out every shred of energy. I want to check my pockets, but there's nothing, not even a crumb. I start imagining I can get through the roof to the canteen and down behind the kitchen grilles. There must be buns and bakeries down there, stuff they got in for the school day, doughnuts and sandwiches and bottles of cool orange juice.

I daren't move. They'll hear me. Even in this light, they'll see me.

'Get back here then,' shouts Damian. 'We'll get a posse out.'

Get a posse out? I got to get back to the toilets. I got

196

to get supplies. I got to find Anton. I need to check on Ruby. She's probably dying of hunger too. What about the bomb? What about Aliesha? I can't get back to her. Even if I could, she ain't got no proper mouth left to chew or swallow nothing. I want to cry about that, cry about the way she ain't going to care about lip gloss no more. Cry and cry, cos I don't understand it. I'm going to do all that. How am I? How am I going to stop that bomb? With a posse out?

Across the ceiling, only five or six struts away from me, one of the shooters is moving nearer. He's grunting as he heaves towards me. I'm feeling so faint, I don't know what I can do about anything. He huffs a bit. I can tell, he don't find walking on the struts easy. It's hard to keep a clear head. First time you're up here, you've got to just lie on them to stop yourself feeling dizzy. He ain't got no head for heights, I'll bet. Probably every glimpse through them fractured ceiling tiles is freaking him bloody out. I pray it's freaking him out. I bite down on my finger. I pray he'll stop and give up. Go back. But he ain't giving up. He's huffing and puffing. He's getting nearer and nearer. I can't bear it. I must bear it. Stay as still as a speck of dust. Shrink into myself. I'm sweating. My palms have gone all slippery. I hold my breath, sucking in air very slowly through my mouth. Don't faint,

197

Leah. But I feel like fainting. I can't even turn my head to look. I just wait, wait for the spray of bullets.

And he comes past me and I can't help it. I let my breath out in a rush of air. And I'm crying for myself. And he turns. And he raises his gun.

And it's Connor.

# 3.45 p.m.
## Friday, 18 September

We look at each other through the speckled light. His eyes meet mine. His mouth drops open. His shoulders sag a bit. He clamps his mouth up tight. He squares back his shoulders. He lifts his gun higher.

'Connor,' I whisper. I look at him. I hold my breath. It's Connor. The same Connor I look at across the kitchen table. 'You ain't really going to shoot me?'

He looks confused, like he's got to think for himself for the first time since all this happened. He don't say nothing, but his chin slacks up a bit. I take in a sip of air.

'It's me,' I say, like stating the obvious will boost that slight slackening in his face. But it's more than just me. It's *me*, the one who does the house and takes care of Mum, who did his duties for him this morning, who fixed his stupid breakfast. *Me, Leah*, who reads stories to Sally, who covers for him when he's done the next stupid thing on his long list of stupid things, it's *me, Leah, his*

199

*sister.* Doesn't he get it? If I ain't around the whole bloody family's had it.

'You're dead,' he says. And I don't know if he means I should be dead, as in a Coca-Cola-bottled-missile strike, or I'm going to be dead, as in he's going to shoot the brains right out of me, right here and now.

'I ain't dead yet,' I whisper. 'You don't have to kill me.'

Connor looks around like Damian is standing over him, ready to cancel the order or insist he carries it out.

'You don't have to,' I repeat.

Then I take a chance because his face is slackening a tiny bit more.

'All this ain't what it seems,' I say gesturing at the gym beneath.

He lifts his jaw up and screws up his forehead.

'Damian is getting help from outside,' I say, making a wild guess, the guns, the ammunition, the walkie-talkie radio comms.

Here Connor's face screws up even more. He kind of snorts. 'I know *that*. It's bigger than you, Leah, and you're in the way.'

'Hey,' I say. I made a mistake going in that direction. 'Look,' I say. I point at the package of explosives wired to the beam. '*Did you know about that?*'

Connor peers forward and the dumb slack look crawls back across his face.

I don't offer no explanation. I used to do that, but you can't explain nothing to Connor. He's got all his own ideas and he don't change them. He stands there swaying on the struts, like he ain't sure no more. Obviously no one told him about that part of the plan.

I push home my small advantage. 'Think about Mum,' I say. 'You can't kill me.'

Suddenly Connor shrugs, like thinking about anything got way too boring for him. This is it, he ain't going to decide to do nothing. I got to ride this now.

'So I'm going,' I say.

I pick myself up and out of the alcove while he can't be bothered about nothing. I start limping off across the struts. I find I can bear the pain in my leg; it's the look on Connor's face I can't bear. The fact he didn't seem to care about saving me; the fact that he could have shot me too, and it would have been all the same to him.

And I move fast. I fly over those struts before he can change his mind, before someone else comes up to check what he's up to, to check why they ain't heard no shots. None of them are going to guess it's because he met his own sister up here. I wonder if he's going to tell them, if my invisible state is going to end, if they're going to start hunting me again. And I don't know. He might. But if he did, he'd have to explain why he didn't shoot me. I'm not sure he can work all that out. He don't know why he didn't shoot me. But he's got a kind of cunning for all that, which goes: if I don't say nothing, then nobody can't know nothing. I figure that's what he'll do. But I ain't sure.

And I didn't tell him about Active Shooting Doctrine. And I'm glad. And I'm glad that I'm glad. I'm growing up. I don't always have to watch out for Connor, do I?

I don't mean to but I stop and look back. Just to check he's OK.

But he ain't there.

He ain't following me.

He ain't gonna shoot me after all.

I'm beginning to feel faint. I got to find food. I got to eat. I got to find Anton. I never ate no breakfast and last night there weren't no food in the house. I gave the leftovers in the fridge to Connor and Sally. I got to eat something. I got to find Anton.

I scout below me, every section of ceiling. I lift a tile to see where I am. I'm hoping the loft space might stretch above the kitchens. I'm hoping I can drop down and raid the sandwiches, but it don't happen. It ain't going to happen. I'm going to have to get into the corridors and try to raid the kitchens that way. And I know I won't be able to. The metal roller blinds on the service hatches will be locked down. The doors have steel grille gates across them. In Challenge Academies everyone knows third-tier kids are always hungry. Hungry and dishonest. They build the place with that in mind.

Why precisely did they build them? I remember Anton's question. *'Have you ever wondered what exactly the role of YOU OP Challenge Academies are?'* I try to wonder what 'exactly' the government might have had in mind. Was it just to keep us off the streets? Offer us a basic education? Contain us so they know they have all the problems in one bag? If they could have got away with *not* educating us, would they have bothered with third-tier kids at all, bothered with YOU OP Academies? After all, education is expensive. Everyone wants a return on their money. The good schools all went private years ago, even the so-called free schools became as private as the public ones. I don't know. I don't know nothing. Except that I hate Volunteer Programmes. If I have to go to one of them, I think I *would* rather be dead.

I give up thinking. I give up thinking about what might be in the kitchens too. I get back down in the girls' toilet. I sit for a long time on a closed loo seat, breathing, trying to catch my heart, trying to return it to its normal rhythm.

I got to do something about my leg. I stand up. I open the tap. I hoist my leg up over the basin and unknot the T-shirt. It's a mess. There's a wound twelve centimetres long stretched right down the flesh of my calf. Gritting my teeth, I wash it. I even soap it. I make sure the water cleans out everything. It hurts like hell. My eyes water all by themselves and I ain't even crying. It starts bleeding a bit. I don't want it to go bad. I go bad at the slightest thing. Not enough fresh food, that's what my Young Carer worker says. I grit my teeth. It stings like you fell in a bed of nettles, but I don't stop. I scrub it gently until all is clean pink flesh with whitish lips. Then I wash out the T-shirt. I tear it into strips. I'm tempted to dry it under the hand dryer, but that's going to make noise so I wring it out as best I can. I bind my leg up. I try testing it. I put my foot to the ground, I try flexing the muscle. I don't try again.

I go and sit on the loo seat. I wipe my eyes with toilet roll. I try to think about what I got to do now. I text Victoria. I write: **They wired the gym – there's a bomb there. It's going to blow – I don't know when. I got you footage of the bomb. It'll cost more if you want it**. I save the footage of the explosive package to a zip file on the

Internet, ready to send to her, safe in the cyber-sphere should anything happen to me. It's safer like that. I download the password to my account in the Cloud.

She don't send nothing back, so I just carry on sitting there. I wasn't going to send it her anyway. If she's right about the government being behind all this, and she puts my footage of the bomb on the news, they'll blow us all sky high straight off.

BOOM.

# 4.00 p.m.
## Friday, 18 September

I pull out the comm. I scroll through it looking for Anton's number. I'm that desperate. But this comm ain't got *no* numbers in it. I knew before I started it weren't going to have his. But it's strange that it don't have *any* of Brandon's numbers in it, neither. It's a brand-new straight-out-of-its-cellophane-package comm. It ain't got no history and no numbers. That's clever. No numbers – no history. Bloody clever.

I think about going on the Net and networking Anton, but that's too risky; if somebody provided Brandon with this comm, they could be tracking or checking up on their investment. At any point they, whoever-they-are, could locate my network. At any minute they could switch on my GPS and pinpoint me. Being Brandon it'd be OK to be anywhere, because he's still out on so-called patrol. Anywhere except in a girls' toilet.

Already there's two missed calls from Damian. And a text. I read it. **Posse out. Meet up on top corridor.**

**Complete sweep through entire building. Some kids still out there. Kill on sight.**

I stare at the comm. I stare at it some more. Finally I turn it off and shove it in my zip pocket. They're going to be up there in the ceiling and out there in the corridors looking for me now. And I'm going to have to come out of the toilet and get back into the library somehow. I'm going to have to climb the shelves again and hoist myself back into the ceilings and find Anton.

We're both going to have to move. I need to get there soon. I need to get there and warn him. They're going to find him too if I don't.

I refill my water bottle. I splash my face, washing away everything, that's how I like to think of it. I've survived this long. I squint at myself in the mirror. I'm not going to die now. I ain't ready to let them win. I don't know what the hell it's all about, but sometimes you don't have to know, you don't have to sit like a poxy magistrate and weigh up whether the defendant had lousy parenting or nothing, you just know it ain't right and it ain't going on – not if you can help it – and that's all.

I test my leg, hold my stomach. I'm so bleeding hungry. I feel shaky. I'm going hyper. My heart's going so fast. It's all fluttery. I want a chocolate nougat bar.

A chocolate nougat bar.

Suddenly I get a brainwave. My brain *is* working.

The chocolate slot machines on B corridor where the Eternals emptied their first round of ammo. I bet to high heaven they bust the mechs wide open. There'll be chocolate bars exploding out of that machine along with Coke cans and crisp packs. I don't stop to figure out more. How can I get there?

I open up the girls' toilet door with the large press green buzzer. I step into the empty corridor. I'm grinning. I got a boiler suit with three good-sized pockets and a grin stretched across my bony old skull. I'm going to get us some choco, Ruby, I say to her. You're going to get that choco what you always wanted.

Out on the corridors though, I don't take no chances. I flit like a shadow from door alcove to door alcove. I duck behind lockers. Slide along walls. The CCTV is always trained on certain places like the fire alarms and the swing doors. I avoid them.

You wouldn't believe it, but kids get a whole kick out of punching out fire alarms. They still do it even though it don't effect Lock Down one bit no more. They ain't even realised that, probably. They don't know that now you gotta have massive amounts of carbon dioxide before the alarms will go and the doors'll open. They just punch them anyway. Like in the old days when it gave them control – got teachers to stop teaching, until it got turned off. Kids like that. They like to do the swing door in your face trick too. Barge through and hold it open, just until you're smack in line for a broken nose, and then woo, shove and wham-smack, and what a fricking laugh that is.

But the CCTV don't show everything. So I continue pressing my back flat against the wall and sidestepping my way down the corridor. My heart is going, but not like before. Connor ain't told on me yet. I can't work Connor out. I've tried. Even as I press myself tight against the wall and slide-step down the corridor, I can't work him out. All I can work out is a shed load of nothing.

Like why would you want to join a gang led by a psycho like Damian? And even if you did join his stupid gang, why would you trust him, when you know he gets off on guns and killing? And even if you did trust him, wouldn't you actually stop and question why the heck you were doing it all anyway? If you wanted to live that kind of life?

I would.

I don't get why the Eternals are doing this at all.

I guess I'm just different. I want to feel my life has some kind of meaning. I reckon only other people can give your life meaning. Other people who need you. I like being needed. You've got to be there for others. You don't have to kill them. Do you?

Up ahead I see the glass from the chocolate dispenser all scattered across the floor. I'm right, it *is* bust open. But to get the chocolate out I'm going to have to risk being picked up by the CCTV. I pause, poised in mid step. How long will it take to get someone from the gym up here? Do I want them to know it's me? Do I want to rise from the dead? And I figure I don't. So I hitch my collar up and drag it right over my head until I just peep out through the front. Then I move forward again. It wouldn't fool Mum and it sure wouldn't fool Sally. It wouldn't even fool Connor, but if he ain't said nothing yet, as sure as hell he ain't going to be squeaking now. You can tell people, you know, by the way they move, that's what I mean. But nobody will know it's me. Nobody's studied me move, have they?

I reckon I got twenty seconds before the CCTV picks me up by the machine, and about four minutes until the Eternals arrive. They're going to arrive quicker maybe, because they sure looked bored before. I pray to heck there ain't broken glass inside the dispenser's shelves, because I'm going to have to scrabble around blind, with my hand up to my armpit reaching in.

I don't hesitate to find out if I got enough nerve to do

this. I don't. I just think we're going to have to eat. I got to take Ruby something better than poxy hope this time and I go for it. I march right up to that machine and it don't matter the hell how much noise I make, so I don't bother. I yell out, '*You're all stupid morons*,' but then I don't yell again, because they can also recognise you by your voice and maybe World Channel News have already hacked into the CCTV and I'm being podcasted everywhere all over the planet.

I kneel down by the choco machine and pull the sleeves of my shirt over my hands. I stick my arm inside it. I swish around for a few seconds and identify a can. I swoop it out and stick my arm in again. Something's rustling. It could be crisp packets, so I hook them out too, but the packet has been shot through so many times all the crisps spill out and I'm left holding plastic.

I stick my hands in a third time and come up lucky. Three bars of toffee nougat crunch. Can I try again? Have I got time? The thought of all that choco still lying in there is too much. I stick my arm in for another go. This time I really get the bull's-eye. One bumper bar of solid milk and white swirl. That's it then. I don't risk my luck or my fingers another time. I straighten up my leg, a spasm of pain screams down into my foot and up into my groin. I stumble. Then I hear the rattling, I hear the windows going like an army of them have just come out the gym, swinging those old swing doors like billy-oh. They're looking for fun, and they're busting right through to my level to find it. I put the choco in my pockets.

Time to go.

I slide back against the wall. I need to disappear from the CCTV. I need to hurry. But my leg is complaining now and I can't put no weight on it. I try sliding in a kind of hoppy motion and it don't impress me at all. I try to imagine what's going to happen. How many of the Eternals are going to come blundering down the corridor? Hell, I wish I still had the gun. You feel so much safer with a gun.

At the rate I'm moving, they're going to catch me long before I get into the library ceiling. Even the ceiling won't offer a lot of protection now they know you can hide up there. They probably haven't figured out about the Lock Down on the girls' toilets though. They've probably just assumed that as they can't get into them, no one can. I can still go there and rest and not worry. At least, not so much.

What I really need is to slow them down. I feel the choco bars bumping around in my pocket. I get an idea. Glass and chocolate. What a great combination. Third-tier kids are always hungry. Instantly I turn. I retrace the distance I've made. I get back to the machine. I drag my boiler collar back over my head and then with one almighty heave I pull the whole dispenser towards me. It rocks. I'm going to have to do much better. I heave again. I put my bad leg up against the wall and shove. It tips. I feel the machine rock. I give it one last tug and then I jump.

Down crashes the dispenser, down on to the tiles. The back buckles, the rest of the shot-out front buckles, the sides tear and screech and split. Suddenly there's glass spraying the corridor and cans rolling down it and packs of five-star nut, and crisps, and iced white dreamers sailing through the air. The whole corridor section is laced with sweets and sodas and glass, and that big old dispensing machine is lying across it, like a totalled jack-knifed truck.

Decoy in place.

Time to go.

# 4.11 p.m.
## Friday, 18 September

I never knew Connor pass by a sweet laid out on a table, or a crisp pack half open on the breakfast bar. I reckon that Brandon didn't get so overweight by saying no to choco. I reckon Jase and Markel are going to stop and pick up every bit of booty they can before they give chase. And even if they don't fancy peanut crunch, they're going to have to pick their way round the glass unless they want to slice up their new trainers. It's going to seriously slow them down.

I turn. I test my leg. It's going to have to hold. I step to the edges of the CCTV view and like a shadow I'm gone. I'm down the corridor again, down the stairwell and out on to the wide Crossing that leads to the library.

By the library door I crouch. Before I open up the book cupboard, I got to be seriously 110 per cent sure nobody followed me. I press myself under one of the desks. It's a desk that the Year Sevens hid under. I pull out a bar of choco caramel and nougat. I unwrap it so

214

very carefully. Not even one bit of crackly wrapping gives me away. And that is not so easy. It takes time. But I got a little bit of time now. Because I am not going anywhere near the book cupboard, not until I'm sure I'm not leading no one to Rube.

I cram the bar into my mouth and start at the way my saliva spurts out into the back of my throat. I didn't know you could get so hungry. I let the chocolate warm in my mouth and melt under my teeth, until I'm really sure I can bite a bit off without a snap or a crack that'll give me away. It's a kind of glorious torture waiting to bite.

My mouth floods with saliva. Finally I sink my teeth into the softened bar. I suck the nougat pieces, I wonder why I don't take some to Aliesha. I find my mind twisting and weaving and saying stuff like: it's too long now, way too dangerous to get back to Lab One. When I think about it, it probably is, but as long as I can lose those morons behind me, I could do it. Heck, I've survived all day and been everywhere. I could get back to Aliesha. I get a sudden sugar-rush and I feel giddy, happy even. I could get anywhere. Then I find myself thinking: she can't eat nothing though, her face is a mess. But she sipped the water OK, and if I melted the bits of chocolate in my fingers and broke them into bits she could do it. She could swallow and it would do her good. So I ask myself then, why Ruby? Why take the chocolate to Ruby and not Ali? And I don't know the answer. I ain't never bothered to ever think like that before. You know, why this? And not that? And why not and all.

I carefully suck the next bit of choco. I tell myself Ruby's got a chance. And Ruby is going to be so happy to get the choco. Ruby always had a chance. Ruby tried to help herself when we was building the table tower in the library. She's going to smile and clap her hands when I show her the big bumper swirl bar. It weren't her fault she didn't make it to safety. It was mine and Anton's and I owe her. Heck, Ruby is going to be so pleased to see me and choco together. Ruby's going to be ecstatic. And she got more spirit than Aliesha anyway.

But I know deep inside that ain't good enough. I should take Aliesha something too. So I take the choco out of my mouth and very carefully fold the bits of paper back around it. I put it, my half-eaten piece, back in my pocket. I'm going to save it for Aliesha, although I don't know when I'm going to give it her, because after I get some to Ruby, I got to find Anton. And he's going to be hungry too. And then there's the bomb. The bomb that could go at any minute. After all, it sure weren't programmed to blow up party balloons.

And that's another thing. How far will the blast reach?

I wonder if it will take out the library. Will it? How safe are we here? I stand up. I peer round the corner of the computer desk.

Nobody.

Good. Crouching low I make it to the book cupboard door. I punch in the combination. I slip out the key and unlock the door. I ease it open. I slip inside. I shut it carefully behind me.

I poise myself in the darkness.

'Ruby?' I whisper. There's a huge smile in my voice.

There ain't no reply.

'It's me, Ruby,' I whisper. 'I got you a surprise!'

I pull out Brandon's comm. And turn it on. There's the beanbag where I dragged it. There's Ruby. She's lying just like I left her.

'You're gonna love it,' I say.

'Leah?' I barely hear the whisper. It sounds like it's coming from a really long way away.

My smile fades. Suddenly my heart starts up thudding to a new awful beat. This ain't the beat of fear – this is the horror of something much bigger. '*Ruby?*' I whisper.

She stirs a little, reaches out her hand towards me. She ain't touched the water I gave her. She ain't moved.

There's something in her voice that freezes my blood. I drop all thoughts of choco. I look at the comm in my

217

hand; who can I call? I ought to be able to call someone? But there ain't no one. If they can't get me out, and I'm well and strong, how're they going to get a team of paramedics in to help her? And it ain't fair, she's hung on so long and she's lain here in the dark when she's so scared of it. I don't know what to do.

'I'm here, Ruby,' I say, and I catch up her hand. It's cold. It's as cold as ice, like she's already dead, like she died hours ago.

'I got you choco,' I say and I pull out the bumper bar of cream white swirl like there's some magic in an ordinary thing that can stop time, stop death. I hold it up, like it's this big red stop flag.

She don't say nothing. I don't know what to do. I don't know if I should give her the chocolate or the water.

'Leah,' she whispers again. I go for the water. I drop the chocolate. I fumble with the screw top. I try to trickle some into her mouth but my hand is trembling and I slosh it on her face. 'I'm sorry. I'm so sorry,' I say, furiously trying to dab the water off with my sleeve, but it's no good. Her face is like ice.

'Ruby,' I say, 'don't die, you hear?'

'Yes,' she says.

But she says it so softly I can hardly hear her.

I want to say other things, like it's going to be OK;

you're going to make it, but I can't. I can't say anything hopeful. Instead I say, 'I didn't make it out.' And then I know that was the most wrongest thing to say, because she ain't going to make it out either. So I try to make it better. 'They didn't get me out,' I say. I'm about to say about Brandon and the bomb, and the way the police are doing things, how I don't understand any of it, but I stop.

'Don't leave me,' she says.

'No,' I say. I pull myself up closer to her. I should have come sooner. I hold her hand. It's so icy, but I need to hold it. I need to hold on to her. If I can hold on to her tight enough, she ain't going to die. I squeeze her hand and I say, 'I'm not going nowhere,' and I bite my lip.

'You tell them about me,' whispers Ruby. I sit there, tears tight in my throat. I think about what I could tell about, how she was little and kind, and shared her lunch with Sally when everyone else didn't, and how it weren't her fault she wasn't rich and couldn't go to a better school. How she mattered even though Anton pushed her out of the ceiling, how she got shot by accident, sort of, and how that was just like her whole life – everything happening just because, without no meaning. I sit there. I think: *I ought to switch the comm off – they might hack into the GPS, if by now they realise Brandon's dead and I'm not.*

Ruby's scared of the dark. She's lain in it all day without crying, and she's going to a darker place now, so I ain't going to turn that comm off, not for nothing.

'I'm so cold,' she says.

I try to get closer to her but I'm scared. I might jog her. It might hurt her more. It might start the bleeding back. So I sit there, and I hold her hand, and I stroke her head, and I lay my cheek against hers and I think about the chocolate, and I try not to cry, and my voice is all croaky.

'Pray for me,' whispers Ruby.

And I remember that she wore a little gold cross around her neck. I ain't got no time for religion, but I ain't got no time anyway, so I rub her poor cold hands and sit up a bit like I'm trying to respect God, and I start with the prayers I know, which ain't many because nobody ever prayed with me.

*'Now I lay me down to sleep, I pray the Lord my soul to keep, and if I should die before I wake, I pray the Lord my soul to take.'*

And my voice is breaking and I don't know no other prayers, so I say it over again.

*'Now I lay me down to sleep, I pray the Lord my soul to*

*keep, and if I should die before I wake I pray the Lord my soul to take.'*

Ruby's little eyes are shut. She's hardly breathing. Her lips move. At first I think she's saying the words with me, but she's not. She's trying to say something. I bend down again to hear what she's saying. My tears drop, because I can't sniff them back down my nose. They roll out. I try to wipe them away but they fall on her anyway.

I bend down to catch what she's saying.

'I'm sorry,' she says.

And that's it. She don't say nothing else. I sit there shaking, and she's gone, and the last thing she said was: 'Sorry.'

Sorry?

Sorry for what? Sorry for dying? Sorry for being so little, for being shot, for leaving me, for being a bother, for being at all? I start to shake and shake, like the bullets and the shooting never made me ever shake before. And I sit there and then I snap out the comm. If she's got to go into the dark, then I'm going to be in the dark too. I sit there and it's like I'm so angry. My anger fills up the whole cupboard and it's big enough to bust open the whole library. I just sit there shaking and shaking and refusing to let go of her hand.

And that's when I know they ain't going to win. They

ain't never going to win while I'm here. I swallow all my anger back inside and it forms a lump of cold ice, right in the pit of my stomach. I don't care whatever is going on, nothing was worth Ruby dying. I take the chocolate bar and I break her off a piece and I hold it in my hand until it's soft and warm and sticky, and then I put it between her lips. She's going to get her chocolate. I press her small dead fingers around the rest of the bar. I stand one bottle of water up like it's standing guard over her. I pocket the other. Then I stand up too.

I call up Victoria.

I say, 'I'm ready to do anything now. You find out what and then you let me know.'

And I am.

# 4.29 p.m.
## Friday, 18 September

I reckon my trick with the choco dispenser kind of worked. I reckon it did, because I got time to scale the bookcases and lift up a ceiling tile and make it back into the library ceiling. I'm not kidding myself it's safe any more; I don't think it is. I think, even though Jase is a stupid moron, he's going to work it out. And if he can work it out, they all can. They're going to get here soon.

Where's Anton? I got to tell him. It ain't safe here any more. Nowhere's safe. We've got to keep moving. When he's trying to work out the less risky option, he's got to figure that in. Everything is equally risky now.

And there he is sitting squeezed up in the same place I left him this morning, waiting. I don't know what he's waiting for. Must be obvious by now we ain't going to be rescued. We're on our own.

'Ant,' I say.

He looks at me.

He raises his head. I can't see what he's thinking. The gloom is too much.

'It's bad.' I shake my head. I can't believe it.

He don't answer me.

'There's a bomb.'

He still ain't saying nothing, so I nudge him with my foot.

'What're we gonna do?' I say.

'You're back,' says Anton, like that's all that matters, like he thought I was a ghost or something.

'There's a bomb,' I say. 'It's in the gym. It's got this digital screen. I thought . . .'

'What does it look like?' he says.

I show him the footage of the bomb.

'Can you hack into it?' I say. 'Can you do anything?'

He don't reply, but he gets his comm out and flicks it on.

'Anton,' I say. 'I don't get it. I think they're going to blow everyone up. They ain't coming in to help us. They're showing some news that don't make sense. Have you seen it? Do you get it?'

Anton nods his head like he's been following everything.

'Connor is one of them,' I say. 'I had a gun. I should've killed him.'

'No,' he says. 'He's just mixed up. You can't kill him for that.'

I think about that, about being mixed up, about fear and hurt, about years of resentment. I should have killed him, but I couldn't. I just couldn't. It could all be over by now. I should have killed the lot of them.

'He just got in with the wrong crowd and forgot to be himself, that's all,' says Anton. 'It could happen to anyone.'

'No it couldn't,' I say.

'When you feel like you don't belong, you just fall in with the crowd. It's done really easy,' says Anton. 'He didn't know you don't have to follow the crowd to feel good about yourself. He just never knew.'

I try and think what Anton means. About belonging and not belonging and getting things wrong. Maybe that was it. Maybe I never saw Connor was lost. Maybe if I'd seen he was lost, I could've done something. Let him know something.

'I could try and hack into the bomb,' says Anton, looking up from his comm, 'but I can't do it from this footage. We'd have to go there. I'd have to see it, read the identity numbers on it, if there are any.'

'Could you?' I say.

'If it's not locked by some digi-ray firewall.'

225

'I mean would you?'

'I'm considering it,' he says.

'It's the deal, ain't it?' I remember, you see. I remember what he said:

*I got to survive and I got to do it my way.*

'Not really,' says Anton.

'They know we're hiding out in the ceilings. It's only a matter of time before they check here,' I say. I want to tell him about Victoria and the filming and the shooting and Ruby and the chocolate, and that it's my fault they know about the ceilings, but I can't. It's too much. There's no time.

He lifts his head. 'I know,' he says, like it was inevitable. 'I know.'

I want him to put out a hand and touch me, because I know if he touches me I'll be forgiven. That's what I think. Forgiven for letting them know about the ceilings, for not killing them all when I had the chance, for not knowing Connor was lost, for not putting Number One first, for not saving Ruby, for so many things. But he's just looking at me and looking at me and knowing everything there is to know. And I did what I did. And that's all. I did it whether he touches me or not.

'I thought I knew,' he says. 'I thought I could understand what it was all about . . .' His voice trails away. 'I thought I could understand why,' he finishes up in a dull tone.

I bite my lip. I choke back the ice-cold lump in my stomach. That's where Anton and I are so different. I don't understand. I don't want to understand. There's nothing to understand anyway. Only stupid ideas and stupid guns and stupid bombs.

'I thought it was all about the bigger picture, the role of YOU OP schools and how kids become whatever society makes them become.'

'I think,' I say, 'some kids are just born bad.'

'I think we are all pawns in some huge game,' says Anton.

'Some kids just give problems right from day one.'

'I think it's the way they're raised,' says Anton.

'Like Connor,' I say. 'Even when he was little, he was a fricking nightmare.'

'They never had a chance,' says Anton. 'You get born into a shitty highrise and you go to a shitty school, and even if you got the brains of Einstein you can't go nowhere with them, because you got to pay to go to university and how're you going to do that? Before you can walk you're done for.'

'And how is killing going to help?' I hiss. I'm annoyed now. I don't buy this blame it all on everything else stuff.

And by the way, is he going to help me defuse the bleeding bomb or what?

Anton lifts his head and looks at me through the darkness. 'Why are they doing it, Lee?' he whispers.

'Wake up,' I say. 'Somebody bought those guns and it weren't Damian. It takes planning if you're going to hold up a school, and brains.' I thought Anton was smart. Does he really think those kids dreamed up those guns and armed themselves?

I put my hand on him. 'This is the way I see it,' I say. 'Somebody out there wants to blow up this school. I don't know why and frankly I don't care, because I happen to be in it, and my little brother – who is a moron – is holding a stupid gun and doing stupid stuff because he believes some stupid crap or other he was told.'

Anton frowns slightly.

'Whoever they are,' I say, 'they're manipulating Damian and the Eternals, making them jump around on their little strings. When they get what they want, they're going to fire them up like a bag of old rubbish and me too and all those little kids and those retards in Year Ten and . . .'

Suddenly it's like a torch beam shone full in my face. 'They want to kill all the kids – that's the deal.'

It's not about anything else. It's all about killing the kids.

I stop then and I go cold – as cold as the ice hole in the pit of my stomach. I flick on my comm. I flick it on to the National News. They are hosting a call-in session. There's a panel of eight debating the future of Challenge Academies.

This is it:

OLD WOMAN: YOU OP 78 has been waiting to happen. Nobody wanted to listen, even after the riots.

YOUNG WOMAN: Challenge Academies are spawning grounds for killers. They foster violence; they encourage anarchy; they should be closed down.

MAN IN GLASSES: Without listening to any phoney human rights groups, either.

MAN WITH BEARD: YOU OP kids should be put in detention camps. They're the problem with this society. Even Volunteer Programmes are too good for them . . .

Victoria is right.

I flick the comm off. That's what this is all about. Closing down every Challenge Academy in the country.

At length I say, 'Soon Damian'll work out we're here.'

I know Anton's listening, even though he don't say nothing.

'Let's go and do it then,' I say. 'You want them to win?'

He's still quiet.

'Let's defuse that bomb and get those kids out of the gym, because you know what? If the government don't care about everyone getting blown up, Mrs Strickland, Tilda's mother, does.'

It's a bit random, but Anton thinks about that. About doing something not just for Number One.

'You really are crazy,' he says at last.

'Probably.'

And I know he's thinking about the risks.

'No point in lying around,' I say.

And I know he knows that. I know he knows just what we've got to do.

I lift my head up. He stretches out. We both raise ourselves up into a crouch. He touches me.

And we look at each other in the eye.

We're going to go and defuse the bomb.

# 4.51 p.m.
## Friday, 18 September

The windows start rattling. Those cheap blast-proof plastic windows are fricking rattling again. Something like popcorn is popping. I don't need to tilt my head trying to make it out. They're in the library. They're crashing through the muddle of desks and shit. They know where we are. They're spraying the ceiling with bullets. I'm up and jumping over the struts like I never had no bad leg. Anton is beside me running fast, running fleet.

'The book corner,' I hiss at Anton. The same bloodstained book corner where Ruby got shot. There's beanbags there. We can jump down on to them from the ceiling and roll and not sprain an ankle. There's a door from the book corner to the far corridor. We can take that at a double sprint.

I turn on the spot and leap back across the struts. Anton swings around too. We're running the other way now, across the gunfire. But I know exactly which

231

tile to kick over and exactly where those beanbags are piled up. I'm going to go for it right now, before Jase and Lucas Bobb have a chance to clamber through all the wreckage.

The ceiling space is freckled with thin beams of bullet-holed light. I'm getting so damn used to being shot at, I'm even getting to like this speckly light. I kick out the tile right above where Ruby hid. I vaguely wonder if I live to get out, whether I'll ever bother going to my Five Minutes of Fame and Fortune interview. I vaguely wonder what the frick all those Five Minutes mean anyway, and whether there ever really was any Fame and Fortune on offer to anyone. Like can you really interview someone for five minutes and figure out if they got university potential? It's nuts.

Then I drop. I jump straight through the hole in the ceiling and on to those thick corduroy-covered bags. I roll away as fast as I can. Anton is dropping right behind me. He don't need to land on my head. I'm up on my feet, not even bothering to feel the pain. I don't care if I've started bleeding again. I'm out the side door on to the far corridor, like you ain't even seen me.

Forget about the CCTV. Forget about everything. I just remember one thing: Lucas Bobb and Jase never liked doing PE. I know. Connor told me. They used to hide out at the back of the weights room and smoke. I figure if you never liked PE, and you've been smoking, then you can't run very quick. Speed is what I got and they ain't. Speed and ziggy-zaggy corridors, because they're thinking you can't outrun bullets, and I'm thinking bullets can't go round corners.

I'm doing as many corners as I can. You'd be surprised at just how many corners there are in our school building.

Footsteps crash behind me. Must be Anton. It bleeding better well be Anton. I can hear ragged breath right at my back. Up ahead is the English corridor. When I reach it, I see it's empty. I duck in between the displays, dodging, leaping, twisting. How good a shot can those kids be? The floor is slippy, treacherous. Something booms, pops, shrieks past me. They're shooting again.

Our only chance is to get through the corridor. I topple a pile of books, spin out the lap safes. My lungs are busting. At the far end of English are some stairs. Make for them, round a corner, past doors and toilets.

One chance.

Just run.

Just pray.

Toilets?

I think of my little sanctuary. I look at a wall clock. It's 5.01 p.m. That should be lucky, but it ain't. The toilets all locked down at 3.30. There's no way back into them, not unless through the ceilings.

I sprint. Anton stays with me. If we can't duck inside the toilets, we've got to duck somewhere else. The rest of the English corridor is too straight – that means bullets. There's not much choice. There's no choice. So I pick a classroom. I might as well die in a classroom as in a corridor.

I ain't got time to tell Anton anything, but I wave him on like I got a plan. He's going to make his own choices anyway.

Just run.

Just pray.

Just dart into a classroom. Turn into it. Hit the floor. Hold your breath and pray.

I choose. I dart. I kick open a door.

The door opens. I race in. Anton races in. I lay one finger over my mouth. I push the door shut. Softer than a swish of net curtain. Click. I hit the floor. I lay on the floor, my chest heaving. I don't breathe. Anton hits the floor too. His breath is all raspy and echoey. I look at him and he gets it. He stops breathing.

I try to hold my breath like that, control a tiny bit in, a tiny bit out. I listen. I hear Jase and Lucas catching up.

I listen. My heart stops. They pause. They stop.

'Where'd they go?' shouts Lucas.

'Dunno,' says Jase.

'You missed them.'

'I never.'

'You did.'

'I never.'

'Check the stairs.'

'You check them.'

Footsteps start up.

I got to breathe soon. The world is going black and silver round the edges.

The footsteps. Each step echoes. Have they gone? Are they going? Have they come back? Footsteps, a load of bellowing, some choice explicit words. Footsteps.

They're going.

For now.

I open my mouth and breathe. I swallow air. Try to get my breath back. I tremble. I shake like a leaf. Anton is white. Like paper. We lie there. We breathe. We gasp. We suck in air like drowning fish. Just panting, wheezing, trembling.

After a while I pull out my last bar of choco. I break it in half. I pass Anton a bit. He smiles, kind of like choco was exactly what he was thinking of.

'Water?' he says.

I realise he ain't come down from the ceilings all day. He's still going on whatever he drank at breakfast. That's a lifetime away. I pass him the bottle I took from Ruby.

I put a square of choco in my mouth. I let it melt. Sweat runs into the corner of my lips, mixes with choco. The floor is already sweat-sticky beneath me. 'Be all right now,' I gasp. 'Get into the ceilings now.' I nod towards the bookshelves by the door, as if he ain't worked that one out.

They've really gone. I hear them pounding into the distance. They didn't make very good Eternal Knights, did they? Like the rest of their sad little lives, they're as big a failure at being bad as they ever was at anything. Their yells grow fainter. My heart starts to get back to regular, whatever regular is these days.

As soon as the choco is gone, as soon as I can swallow some water to wash out that gloopy feeling in the back of my throat, I pull on Anton's sleeve. I sign-mouth him to get up off the floor and up on to the bookshelf and into the ceiling again.

And you know, I'm kind of getting the hang of getting into ceilings. I don't think muscles can grow all in one morning, but it's like I've learned the knack of hoisting myself up and in and rolling clean on to the struts. I've grown used to this dim world of ceiling, where it's kind of dusty and smells kind of musty – even though it's not so dusty – or musty – and it's kind of like you get into this mechanical place where it's all bolts and wires. Some bits of the ceiling are tidier than others. Maybe the guys who worked on different sections were different. Maybe some of them were lazy, and thought: *I'll just hook this up here, and get the hell out and all.*

We head for the gym. Anton is surprisingly quick when he gets going. We're both trying not to make any noise. We can't go that quick. It's difficult when we get back to the gym. All the tiles are in a bad state. Some of them have been completely mashed up. All the ones in the centre are peppered with bullet holes. We slow right down to snail speed. We stop at the edge of the gym ceiling. Down there Damian is listening. Must be. He knows we could be anywhere. We must be nuts coming back here. We wait. I start shaking. I *am* nuts. Why the hell am I here?

We set out around the gym ceiling. We're walking a tightrope with each step. It's hard, you know, to balance on a tightrope. My muscles start aching. My bad leg can't take it. I can't bend down to nurse it neither. And I can't make no noise, not even a squeak of shoe leather.

Anton sees I'm in trouble. Like some kind of boy ballerina, he sashays back and holds my hand. Together, hand in hand, we tiptoe around the rim of the ceiling, until we're level with the RSJ beam. It's a bit easier now. You can kind of crouch on the beam, and use your hands to pull yourself along. You've only got to watch out for the support struts, which criss-cross diagonally every other metre or so, down the length of the main beam. You have to get a grip on them and swing yourself past. You've got to be really careful not to send out a foot to balance yourself. After the bullet-spattering these tiles have taken, they're as fragile as soap bubbles. The minute you touch them, they'll fracture and betray you.

We make it to the bomb. I squat, balancing on the beam. Anton leans forward to look at it. I try to control my breathing. The entire rest of the school is below us. They ain't making much noise. They ought to be making a lot more noise. I wish they were. In fact, I never heard the school so quiet before. Usually they're kicking up a row and shouting and hollering and woo-hooing all over, but now, just when I need noise, they're quiet. I listen. All I can hear is Lucas doing his usual patter. I think it's Lucas. If it is, he must've come back. I don't know if that's a good thing or not. At least he's chatting on about something.

Like: 'Shall we get them all to lie down on their faces,

Damian, like at the cult whatever massacre where they all drank poisoned Kool-Aid? If we're going to go down in history, we got to do something big, yeah?' He's quiet for a few minutes. Nobody is talking back to him, so he says, 'Yeah, yeah, you're right – we should be magnanimous,' which he can't even say properly; he makes it sound like 'magnet-mouse'. 'We should treat them with dignity and let them drink water.' And still nobody's saying nothing. So Lucas continues: 'But I ain't going to get them all that water, and we can't let them go to the water fountains to fetch it, so who's going to do the water thing? And then they're going to want to piss on account of the water.' He goes quiet like this is the first time he's ever thought about consequences to anything; like the first time he's ever considered they were human at all.

And nobody else says much, except one of them, who I can't see, but it might be Connor's friend Edison, who says, 'I want a new comm. That's what they got to give me, a new comm and Joe-Joe's Double Whopper burger with Xtra-large fries and curry dip.'

My hand aches from hanging on to the cross beam. Anton works quickly, his head bent over his comm. I try to spy down through the ceiling, through a bullet hole, to see what's going on, but I can't see nothing, only a kid's

239

head and someone moving something. I'm too scared to move closer. I feel sick. My heart is hammering. I can feel it right in my spine.

I hear Anton suck in his breath. I close my eyes up tight. Maybe this is the bit when he has to pull out a wire or something. Then I feel him stiffen. In the darkness he turns to me. 'It's no good, Lee,' he says. 'I can't do it.'

'Can't do it?' I say.

He nods, all the light in his eyes gone. They're like great round dark holes looking back at me.

'Can't do it,' he repeats.

'So,' I mouth. 'What're we gonna do?'

He shakes his head. 'It's automatically configured. If I try to crack it, enter the wrong password, it'll blow. That's the way the default is set. I've tried to reconfigure, but it's linked to a remote computer. I can't get access.'

'Can't you hack the remote?' I whisper.

He shakes his head. 'It's got too many walls round it – it's user identifier access only too. It ain't going to like my eyeball picture – even that might make it blow.'

'What the frick we gonna do?' I say again, looking back at him, and now my eyes are holes too. We're locked into the school. We're sitting on top of a bomb and beneath us is a bunch of Year Nines with guns and no brains, just longing to let air into us.

240

Anton shrugs. He's worried.

I start madly wondering if we can lift a panel on the roof and get out that way, but I know it's stupid to even think about it. When they mean Lock Down they mean Lock Down. The whole school is built like a prison.

'Nothing we can do,' he says.

There *must* be something we can do. I've come a long way since this morning, since I was racing down the humanities corridor towards the fire exit. But I don't come up with nothing, except a picture window on Level A that ain't there no more and has a lot of blood right near it.

Anton swings down from the crossbeam and balances on a couple of struts, looking at me.

His eyes are sucking me into their empty centres. 'It's bad, Lee,' he says.

I look at him. I'm kind of getting used to shocks. 'Just tell me,' I say. 'Can't get much worse, can it?'

Anton carries on looking at me. He touches my shoulder, but it ain't a flirty kind of touch, nor an encouraging one, neither. It's just a touch, like one human being to another when there's nothing left to do.

'What?' I say.

'They can detonate it any time,' he says.

'They?' I say.

'Yeah. Whoever's planted it can set the bomb off any time.'

I nod because I kind of figured that anyway. 'So?' I say.

'It's a very clever, smart bomb.'

'So tell me,' I say.

'This bomb looks home-made – crap digital set-up, off-the-street explosives – but it ain't. It's configured to look like the kids planted it. If it goes off there'll be no evidence to show otherwise.'

'If it don't?' I say.

'It can also implode and look like a botched job.'

'I see,' I say. I don't really.

'It's very powerful. When it goes, it'll take out the whole gym. All that.' He points at the benches. All the kids. All the staff. 'And probably The Crossing and N wing.'

'Oh,' I say.

'The bad news is there may be others linked by wi-fi to this one. They could be anywhere. They could be everywhere across the school. Setting this one off could start a chain reaction.'

I look at him. I read what he's thinking. Nowhere is safe. There is no less risky choice left.

'But I think this one is the hub. I don't think its range will reach right to the end of O wing, for example.'

Should we go and hide in O wing?

'But I can't be sure.'

Getting all the way to O wing would be pretty risky too.

'Just hope they make it quick then,' I say. 'This waiting is killing me.' I want to raise a smile.

'But it ain't going to be quick, Lee,' he says, like this is the real sting coming. 'I think they're planning on keeping this going all over the weekend.'

I crouch down then and have to reach out, hold on to a crossbeam.

*All weekend?*

And I get it. They're going to be rolling out film about kids killing each other, all weekend. They're going to show how that black-hooded little row of victims gets hanged, drawn and quartered by the vote of other kids right across the globe. They're going to ratchet up the public so much that everyone's going to be screaming about it, and by the time Negotiations Break Down and they 'Rush' in to save us, everyone's going to be very ready to believe that Year Nine kids could do this, all on their stupid own and then blow themselves up too. And if the public moan about Why The Armed Forces Didn't Storm The Building Fast Enough the thing that will really stick will be the kids. The Dangerous Anti-social Feral Kids.

And you don't need a university degree to tell you what'll happen next.

Little Sally won't never go to school after primary. She'll be threading chips on a production line, she'll be graduating from a Volunteer Education Into Industry Programme.

Suddenly I start to feel really hazy. The ceiling looks like it's rippling. Like it's a great sea unfreezing itself and starting to move again. I can see it lapping at the distant shores of the walls. I sway a little and reach down towards my leg. I should have tightened the bandage. I can feel the sticky trickle of blood down my calf. I try to bend to sort it but a rush of vertigo catches me and I topple.

My hands go out in front of me, and the last thing I remember is a speck of dust whirling like cherry blossom, falling through a beam of light from a bullet hole.

# 5.32 p.m.
## Friday, 18 September

The sound of a curious thumping, like the dustbin being emptied outside my window back home, slowly pulls me awake. I'm sluggish. I don't want to get up and put the rubbish out. I try to turn to get my head back into the pillow, but I can't turn. I'm all tangled up in the sheeting. An indistinct aching in my head and leg nags away at me. I try to unwind the sheeting. It must be the weekend, that's why I've slept late. Although it's still dark out, I blink to be sure. A spider's web shines in the moonlight. Yes, it's still much too dark to wake up. Mum is here. I can feel her holding me and stroking my hair. I vaguely know that something must be wrong, because Mum never strokes my hair. She stopped holding me long since. I miss that. I suddenly realise I miss all that touching and holding and caring. I lie very still, so I won't scare her away.

'Lee?' says my mum, but her voice is all wrong and my eyes fly wide. In a moment I'm on high alert, thinking someone just broke into the house. The spider's web flies out. The dream is shattered. I'm lying along the main beam in the ceiling of the gym. I'm shivering. I try to move, but now I realise Anton has belted my legs to the beam and is holding my torso in his arms.

'Hey?' I say. Everything floods back. 'It never went off?' I say.

Anton just strokes my head. He looks down at me and his eyes aren't holes any more.

'There's an up-side to everything,' he whispers.

I don't quite get it, but I relax back into his arms. I feel his thumb running over the side of my face. I like it.

I lie there for a while trying hard not to remember the morning. Ruby. Brandon, that boy by the window. The three little Year Sevens in the library. Aliesha's face.

I look up at Anton to try and read his expression, if there's any better news. But I know there ain't.

'You fainted,' he says. 'You nearly went through the bloody ceiling.'

I wonder vaguely how he saved me. Did he leap to his feet, straddle the struts, fling himself forward to catch me?

I smile.

'Had to belt you in,' he says. 'You've lost a bit of blood. Your T is soaked.'

I nod. It's all academic now, how much blood I lose; how much blood I have lost; how much blood I will lose.

Anton reaches out and holds my hand. I let it lie there in his. I don't even know what to think. I don't know *how* to think – about this – this tender reaching out in the middle of so much violence. So I just lie there, and for once I don't have to know everything. I don't have to rubbish anything. For once maybe I can let myself just not know.

Anton holds something up to my lips. It's the choco. I smile. He saved a piece for me. He puts it gently in my mouth. Its sweetness floods my throat. A sudden rush of saliva. But more than the choco sweetness, is the sweetness of lying there near him.

'I've been taking care of you,' he says, stating the obvious. And I nod, responding with the obvious too.

Neither of us says what we're going to do. Neither of us says what we're thinking. We don't say nothing. We just stay that way, smiling.

Maybe outside it's a sunny day and kids like us are lying somewhere beside a river, soaking up the sun, maybe skinny-dipping and laughing, maybe splashing about a bit. I wish I was there. I close my eyes, trying to feel the sun by that river warming me. I look up into a really blue sky, watching a few birds diving around and soaring back up. The tops of trees are swaying and that smell of summer's everywhere. Lying around on an endless summer afternoon in that land somewhere.

But I know I ain't there. Even if I was there and Anton weren't, it wouldn't be no fun. And even if we was there, some yobs, as likely as not, would come scooting down the banks and shouting and throwing stones into the water. Then they'd open up some music and blast away the birds and the breezes with Shoot-Up-the-Gangster rap, and if we sit up or look at them dodgy, like we wasn't enjoying having them around, they'd come right up and stuff their faces in front of us and say, 'What's your effing problem?' and like as not one of them would have a knife.

So I let the sunny riverbank picture fade to black. I'm back in my ceiling, strapped to the bomb beam, in Anton's arms. And I look at him and you know, there's dreaming and there's reality. It's always a good thing not to get the two muddled up.

'So I'm going,' I say.

'Going?' he says.

'Yep,' I say. 'This is nice and all, but we can't lie here the whole weekend and you know it. Sooner or later one of us will have to try and raid the choco machine again, or see if we can get into the kitchen and then they're going to hear us, or see us, and a posse of morons are going to set out after us again. You know it. I know it. So I'm going.'

He laughs, like he likes the way I express myself. 'Going where?' he says, as if he's imagining me strolling out of the building and going right on home.

I jerk my head. 'Only one place to go now,' I say.

'Yeah?' he asks, like I've outfoxed him this time.

I roll my eyes in the direction of the gym. 'I'm going down there, of course. It's the only logical thing left to do. We can't get past Lock Down. We ain't gonna get rescued. We can't defuse the bomb. Only one thing left to do, go down there and politely ask Damian to let us all out.'

# 5.52 p.m.
## Friday, 18 September

Anton looks at me; he's worried. He shakes his head. He's looking more scared than even when he told me he couldn't defuse the bomb.

'No,' he says. 'No way, Lee. I'm not going to let you.'

'Think about it,' I say. 'Damian can reverse Lock Down. It's just a switch in the main office and he's got the remote.'

'He'll shoot you,' warns Anton.

'Well, unless something happens, I'm dead anyway,' I say. I want to add, 'When you got nothing, you know, you got nothing to lose,' because it would be such a good time to say it. But it's a corny line and it ain't the truth anyway. Somebody's always got something to lose, even if it's only tomorrow.

Anton is growing paler by the minute. He grips my hand. I'm almost expecting him to say he's going to keep me strapped up to the beam for ever.

'Think,' I say. 'Damian's only a person. He ain't got

250

supernatural powers. Does he think he ain't going to die like all of us? Maybe he needs reminding. When I tell them about the bomb, about the TV channels and the phone-in debates, hell, nobody wants to die – not for some weird government economy measure, if that's what it is. Even Damian won't want to die.'

'You think?' says Anton. I can see he's weighing it up: is it less risky to appeal to Damian or to try and get to O wing, on the off chance that it's out of the bomb's range?

'I know Connor and he's a yellow-lily-livered rat and so is Lucas Bobb and Jase. They may feel the business with guns in their hands, but they don't know about the bomb, do they? They're only thinking: have fun, play war games, fancy trainers, burgers and ice cream, for frick's sake. They ain't really ready to die for that shit.'

Anton looks a bit more convinced. 'But Damian must be in with the government. He got the guns. Do you think he doesn't know about the bomb? Even if Jase and the others don't?'

'I ain't sure,' I say, 'but I don't think he knows about the bomb.'

'Too much of a risk,' says Anton.

'It *is* a risk,' I say, 'but you can get risks wrong. I bet going to school this morning was a risk you never saw coming. And what else is there to do? Sit here and wait to die? Great. If only even half the kids in the gym believe me, they gonna turn on them, and some may get shot, but if the Eternals turn on Damian, he's gonna get it. How many do you think he can kill before they get him? And then they gonna snatch up the remote and Lock Down is going to end. It's got to. It's got to be like that. That's the only way.'

Anton is watching me. His eyes've gone beyond black holes. 'You can only think like that when it's not you who's going to get shot,' he says. 'I mean, think in statistics and percentages.'

'OK,' I say, getting exasperated. 'Tell me your plan then.'

But Anton ain't got a plan, so he says nothing.

Then he nods his head as if he'd figured it all out. 'For the greater good, eh.' He smiles as he says 'greater good'. It's a phrase the government like to pump. You know, tighten your belts *For the Greater Good*, go to a Volunteer Programme *For the Greater Good*, support the Big Society *For the Greater Good*.

Shoot your brother *For the Greater Good*.

'But it's true,' I say. 'Even if I die, some of the kids will be going home tonight. Maybe you too.'

'No,' he says. 'No. I can see where you're coming from,

252

Lee, but you're hurt. You can't do this. I'll do it.'

I smile then. And I'm amazed. What came over Anton? What happened to save Number One? 'So you'd like to keep me alive, would you?' I say.

He nods like he'd like that very much.

And suddenly I'm overcome. I'm choked up. Nobody ever cared like that before. Not *that* much. 'Then help me,' I say.

He looks at me like he wants to add, 'But there's no point in two of us getting killed, is there?' But I cut him up short. I want to hold on to this feeling, this sudden rush of something so crazy it makes me want to cry. And I know something then and it's important. I know that there is something beyond just survival. I struggle to frame it in my mind. It's about *how* you survive, it's not about the future or even the present, it's not about bones and blood and staying alive. It's not. It's about something fragile, something lovely that's hidden deep in all of us. Something that makes everything *matter*.

I swallow. I'm only sad that I never knew about that before, that the time I have left may be so short. But it tells me I'm doing the right thing. 'You stay here,' I say. 'When I get to the bit about the bomb, you kick out these ceiling tiles and shine your comm right on it. You shout

out how it really is a bomb. We'll let the Eternals know they've been set up.'

Anton almost nods.

'Then jam the airwaves when I say. Can you at least do that?' I say, almost smiling.

'I can jam them,' he says.

'Good enough so they can't remotely detonate the bomb?'

'Good enough,' he says.

'For how long?'

'Maybe five minutes, not more.'

'OK, five it is.'

He nods.

'Then bingo,' I say.

'Bingo?' he says.

I loosen Anton's belt around me. I straighten up. As I try to stretch out my injured leg I see something lying on the far side of the beam. It shines in the dappled gloom. It's the gun.

'We've just struck lucky,' I say. I lean over very carefully and pull it in towards me. Anton sits there, still looking puzzled.

'Bingo!' I say again and show him.

He takes the gun, turns it over. He taps in numbers on the digital screen. 'Maybe not so lucky,' he says. 'It's only got one shot left.'

Not really enough to take them all out with. We look at each other. I almost laugh at myself, all that soul searching and there weren't even enough bullets anyway. 'Make it count then,' I whisper. His eyes say: Don't worry, I'll make it count.

'Well, here goes nothing,' I shout out.

And I don't stop to ask my heart what she thinks about all this.

I just jump.

# 6.07 p.m.
## Friday, 18 September

I hit the tile above the trampoline and bust through. I raise my arms up, so they won't catch a flying knock on the struts. The polystyrene shatters. I'm through.

I hear gasps, a scream.

The air swishes past. A gun fires. My ears stuff up, go thick, then pop. And I'm falling, trying to get my legs splayed, trying to keep my balance, trying to keep my bad leg crooked a little so when I hit the trampoline I'll catch it with my good one first. It'd be nice to be a showgirl, to do an awesome forward flip, but I'll settle for a safe landing. I'll bounce. I'm going to bounce until I'm sure they've stopped firing. I'll give myself the best chance. I don't think many of them Eternals have had much practice shooting down moving targets.

But there's no more shooting, only Anton's voice. It's loud. He's got some app on his comm that can do him a megaphone. 'Hold your fire. I have a gun.' To underline this he sends a shot straight at Damian. It misses though.

Well, kind of. It just nicks his cheek. He shrieks, drops the gun. It wasn't meant to kill. There's a good lot of blood. It's very dramatic. Why didn't I think of that? A bullet to intimidate. A bully bullet.

Our last bullet.

'A warning,' bellows Anton.

Our one shot gone. Good job Damian don't know that.

I make the most of the drama. I shout out, 'White Flag! White Flag!' But I don't think those Year Nine kids really understand White Flag, so I change. I yell, 'Parlay,' like I'm in *Pirates of the Caribbean*. They all know about Parlay. They've all been watching and playing *Pirates of the Caribbean* since they could crawl.

'*PARLAY!*'

And one of them yells, 'She wants to Parlay,' and his voice is all excited like we're already inside the damn game ourselves.

I've hit the trampoline. My bad leg's buckled. I catch a bounce. I do a forward roll, but it ain't awesome or anything. I'm a bit sad about that, because if you're about to die, it'd be nice to have done it with style. But then I hear them all shouting, '*Parlay! Parlay! Parlay!*' and I know they're going to listen, so I can quit bouncing and say my bit.

So I do. I bend my knees and kill the bounce. I stagger forward and then I stop. I straighten up and despite

Anton's bandages, I know my leg's bleeding again.

'Flipping hell,' one of the Eternals says. 'It's Leah Jackson.'

Five hundred pairs of eyes are fixed on me. And they're all round with surprise, wide with hope, dancing with the reckless, daring thing I've just done. It's like a drug. I feel it, the amazement, the terror, the hope. I didn't even need the awesome forward flip. This is real. I've just made their day.

I'd like to do something to acknowledge their amazement. I'm tempted to give them the victory V or the thumbs-up. There's little Tilda Strickland, her head up at last and she's looking at me like I'm her hero. I'm glad she's smiling. Her mum would be glad.

'You're supposed to be dead,' hisses Damian. He's looking evil. He's dabbing at his cheek, sunk on his king chair, his gun held loosely in his right hand. He ain't pointing it at me though. He's looking all around, but mostly up at the ceiling. He's wondering how many of us are up there, how many guns we've got. If the next shot is going right through his skull.

I nod. 'Yep, that's right,' I say. I know I got to be really careful now, no smart comments like 'You're dead right', no contradictions, no firing up his reactions, because he's so touchy; he ain't stable. I got to get my bit said, and I got to do it in a way that's going to get everyone believing me.

There's this awkward pause. I can see that Damian is about to decide something nasty. I don't want that.

'Wait,' I say. 'Rules of Parlay, you hear me speak.'

Damian don't say nothing, because he ain't playing no *Pirates of the Caribbean* game, is he?

But the Eternals are. One of them says, 'That's right, she's got to speak, and if we don't like it we get to make her walk the plank.'

I see Connor standing away back, as white as a sheet. He ain't saying nothing, just looking around like it is *so* embarrassing to have your sister jump out of the ceiling shouting: Parlay.

'Listen,' I say quickly, before anyone does something unhelpful. 'I come to Parlay, because while I could've saved myself . . .' I pause; I don't let my chin wobble nor my voice waver. They have to believe me. 'While I could've saved myself,' I repeat, 'or taken you all out with a round of bullets . . .' I pause again to let that sink in, to let them know they ain't so damned safe any more, that other folks out there have got guns too. 'I think you all need to know that there's a bomb up there, and it ain't full of bubbles, and it ain't a joke, and it *will* go off and it *will* kill you all, and somebody is taking the piss.'

I let this sink in too.

There's a sigh that runs around the gym. You can hear it. It's like waves on a shore, like the wind down chimneys.

'And if you'll allow me to message you from my comm, to any one of your comms,' I add, careful like, to show Damian I am taking his permission on this, in case he decides to just bullet me there and then. 'If you'll allow me, I can prove it. I can send you footage. I can prove that the bomb in the ceiling is set and ready to blow and that's all.'

There's a silence, a deep silence, like this wasn't expected. The Eternals are all looking at Damian like he wired the bomb or something, like he should've told them. But Damian's looking at me, and I can tell just from that glance that I'm right. Nobody ever told *him* about it neither.

But because nobody ever told him about it, he ain't ready to believe me, not just like that.

'I can prove it,' I say again, but this time it's for Anton's benefit.

And Anton does me proud. He suddenly cracks open five tiles right above us and stands hanging off the beam, and it's like showtime. He's got the torch beam on his comm pointing straight at the bomb. It's all lit up in rainbow-style strobe effect.

It's bloody brilliant.

Everyone turns and looks up. Necks crane. Jaws drop.

There are groans and gasps. A ripple of scraping and scrabbling runs through the gym, short cries puncture the shuffling. And Anton done it good, in such a way that it looks extra. I breathe a little easier, because when you're dealing with kids who can just shoot you through the head for fun, you've got to give everything an extra bit of spin, or you ain't going to get the effect you want.

'Meet Anton,' I say. I try to keep my tone light, friendly, fun even. I know these kids. I know how fragile their sense of self is, how fractured their control. One sign of hostility and they will go into super drive. They'll switch on us. I know. I live with Connor.

Anton catches my mood. He does a twirl, bows to the audience, hold up his gun and says, speaking in his calmest drawl, 'I'd have defused it myself, but someone else's got hold of the detonator.'

There's a murmur then and I can tell the Eternals are thinking: Is this for real? Are they telling it straight? Who wired that bomb? What for? And some of them are thinking: I need to get out. I *so* need to go. And others are thinking: Duh, I don't get it. Who's got the detonator then? And they're looking around like they're going to see the Big Fat Controller holding the Big Fat Detonator with Big Fat Bomb Detonator Control written on it.

Suddenly it all goes deadly quiet.

I turn to the Eternals. I'm taking a risk. Damian won't want to feel his power over the whole show is weakening, but I got to weaken it. I can tell just by looking at him he's mad as hell. He's close to the edge. He don't give a damn. He could shoot me as easy as picking his nose. 'Murder' just ain't one of the words he spends a lot of time worrying over.

But I *got* to get the Eternals to switch sides. So I try to figure out my next move. I reckon, though they might be a gang, they're not Damian's army. They don't follow his orders. Those morons couldn't belong to any kind of army, because they *can't* follow orders. They come from families where Mum and Dad are only shadows. They go to school where they do what they want – which is pretty much nothing. They don't value their education. Hell, they don't even value themselves. They can kick off about the wrong filling in a burger bun but, believe me, they don't even think about vitamins or whether too much sugar's going to rot your teeth.

And these kids Know. Their. Rights.

They know how they're supposed to be treated, and that's where I play my next card.

'You got rights,' I say. 'You can walk out of here, no problem. The bomb may blow your school sky high, but you got rights. Hell, you can probably even get compensation for losing a day of your education.'

And as I say that, it dawns on me about the phone-in. If everyone got their rights but nobody's producing nothing, how's the government going to keep paying up on compensations? Since all those families sued for compensation over the school closures during the last riots, they must be stony broke. Even my mum sued and we got a big cheque. And suddenly I see why it might be better for the government to just close YOU OP Academies altogether. If they did away with free education, nobody would have no rights to nothing. It'd be a lot cheaper.

But Connor and Jase and that lot won't figure that one out, so I carry on. 'You got rights and you got the right not to be blown up, actually.'

They think about that. One of them turns to another and says, 'It's true, we don't have to sit here and get blown up. We got our rights.'

I smile, but only on the inside. I got them thinking. I got them thinking the way I want – that they can do whatever they like: kill and shoot – no problem; intimidate and imprison – easy peasy; and they can still walk out of here alive. Absolutely. In fact they can walk scot free out of every court in the land. Plus get compensation.

I nod. 'Yeah, you can claim duress. You can claim you was forced to do it,' I say.

Instantly I realise the snag. Somebody's got to have done the duressing, haven't they? The Eternals look at Damian. He's holding his face, looking pale. I meet his eyes.

One of the Eternals says, 'But we don't have to say who.'

Damian's eyes are wide and blue.

'We can say "No Comment".'

Wide and blue like snake eyes.

'We got our rights.'

And he's smiling.

So I smile back – my smile says: You've got to make a choice.

- Shoot me and see what Anton will do.
- Take the rap and let us out.
- Get blown up along with everyone.
- Claim you never killed no one and get a lighter sentence.
- Blame someone else.

He narrows up his eyes and squints at me. He's considering a whole new barrage of choices that don't involve none of that.

'So far you didn't shoot nobody, did you?' I say. If I can coax him to believe he ain't done nothing too bad, that he needs to keep it that way, that if he don't shoot me, he could come out of all this squeaky clean.

But he's thinking. And I don't know where his thoughts are going. My heart's thumping. And I don't know what to say next. I drop my gaze. I look at the pile of workout mats he's sitting on. I try not to stare at the Lock Down remote. There it is, lying there, just beside him. It's such a little thing; I wonder how it can hold the fate of so many. I try not to imagine pressing the green button on it. I don't want to let him see. I drag my mind back, but I'm already imagining pressing that button. I'm already pushing down on the door bars, opening up the gym, walking out into the sunshine.

'I mean,' I say, 'are *you* to be blamed for what *they* do?' But I say it in a way – not like, you are so a sad loser who has no control – but like, is it your fault if they go off and do stupid stuff? (Like killing people is just some kind of misdemeanour.)

Damian ain't that stupid though. 'What's your game?' he says, like he knows I got some angle in this.

I throw my hands in the air. I look him straight in the eye and say, 'I dropped in on you guys not because you caught me, or rounded me up or nothing. I coulda stayed in my end in this school, and minded my business. I dropped in on you, because I found a bomb. I figured you might not want to die just yet.'

Damian looks at me. He is unimpressed. 'Leah Jackson to the rescue,' he says, all cold and sarcastic.

'Yeah,' I say. 'Why not?' Like does everything have to have a reason? I can see him thinking. He knows as sure as hell he didn't wire that bomb. He knows I know he didn't. Maybe he thinks I wired it. He don't want his gang to guess he don't know about it though.

Markel steps forward. 'It's a trick,' he says.

'Shut up,' says Damian. He's not happy. His eyes are scanning and re-scanning the ceiling. He's trying to work out how many guns are pointing at him. But telling Markel to shut up was a mistake. Markel turns on him with an ugly look. Damian don't care.

'You'll do what I say,' Damian snaps. 'And if I say shut up – you better shut the frick up.'

Markel's eyes narrow.

Damian scans the ceiling again. Suddenly a slight smile twitches his cheeks.

'Yes, you'll do exactly what I say,' he repeats. He turns to the ceiling. He lays down his gun. He shouts, 'Hey, Anton, listen to this. He's going to do what I say.'

He turns to Markel. 'So do what I say.'

He lifts up his head and points at me.

'Shoot her.'

# 6.22 p.m.
## Friday, 18 September

My blood freezes. I take a step back. I don't believe it. Keep your nerve. Sweat trickles down my back. I look at Damian. I look at Markel. Show Damian and all them Eternals you don't care, not even about a shot in the head. Should I start bouncing again? I don't know. I'm frozen.

Markel raises his gun. He looks at Damian. You can tell from the set of his shoulders he's never going to do what Damian says ever again. I take in a tiny sip of air. Does that mean I'm safe? I can't tell. Markel steps forward menacingly towards Damian. 'Do wot?' he says sneeringly.

Kids stop shuffling, stop sobbing. They straighten up. It goes horribly quiet. Everyone's looking at Damian. What's he going to say?

But Damian is smirking. His cheek has stopped bleeding, and he's back in control. He laughs at Markel. '*Do wot?*' he mimics, like Markel is a retard. Then he looks up at the ceiling, and he gives Anton the finger.

I get it.

267

A chill runs down my spine.

*I get it!*

Damian purposely told Markel to shoot me, to see if Anton would shoot Markel. *But Anton didn't do nothing. He never shot Markel. He didn't shoot nobody.* Now they all know either Anton's a pussy or he ain't got no bullets left.

Great.

Damian just set Markel up.

Damian just set me up.

Damian just set Anton up.

Two little words, that's all it took to turn the tables on all of us. Clever Damian.

Markel sucks at his teeth. He might not be all that with sentences, but he understands it too. He narrows up his eyes. He glances up at the ceiling. He turns to face Damian. '*You . . .*' is all he can manage to stutter out.

Damian smirks.

Markel can't believe it. His eyebrows go up, his jaw drops down.

'*You . . .*' Markel still struggles to find the words.

Damian rolls his eyes like Markel's the slowest kid in an entire nation of retards.

'*You just set me up,*' Markel at last manages. He really can't believe it – that his hero, Damian Phillips, Gun

268

Guerrilla of the Eternal Knights, has just used him up like a spent cartridge.

Damian shrugs.

A void opens up between them. Desperately I try to step into it. My heart's sticking to my ribs. My tongue feels thick and heavy. 'If you flick on the National News you'll see something,' I say. 'They've got footage about a Big Brother murder game.' I don't say that to no one in particular. I'm not telling anyone what to do. I just say it like I told them about the bomb. Like it might be fun to watch. Like all information has got to be welcome.

'*You set us all up,*' manages Markel.

My blood is pounding so hard I feel faint.

A barrage of puzzled looks shoot between the Eternals and Damian.

Lucas says, 'We never saw no news. You said we wasn't to watch it.'

'Yeah,' adds Jase, like that's the most profound thing he can think up to say.

'*You.*' Markel can't believe it. He looks like he's swallowed a bag of nails.

The kids on the benches shuffle forward. Sweat breaks out on my forehead. The teachers start to look interested. One bead of sweat trickles down the side of my face.

'We don't watch the news, because they'll try to get

inside our heads,' says Damian very slowly, like he's talking to morons. 'We agreed that we're making history. We're the Eternal Knights of Darkness.'

'*You just tried to get me killed,*' continues Markel.

'What's on the news?' says Edison.

Connor says nothing. He's just looking at me, looking and looking.

'Mind games,' says Damian.

'Why're you allowed to watch it then and we can't?' says Jase.

Damian gives Jase a look, like that should be obvious. I want to wipe the bead of sweat away. I don't move.

'The news sucks,' says Edison.

Markel is just standing there. He's still looking at Damian. He shakes his head like water got in both ears. '*Mind games?*' he repeats.

'Yeah, what *is* on the news?' says Lucas.

'None of your business,' says Damian.

Suddenly Markel steps forward to the wall where the giant sports screen is. He flicks it on. He touches a channel in. The screen turns blue, warms up and there, stretched across the wide screen, is a new line-up of kids. They all have black bags over their heads and a stupid name written underneath them.

'We're voting on Rottina,' says this voice, scarily like Damian's.

'She's a spoiled brat from Italy who never gave us any of her sweets. She also didn't want to be friends with no one and spoke stupid English. What do you say? If you want to vote for Rottina Coffin getting the chop next, hit the red button on your comms.

'If you've got any creative ideas about how to chop her – message us with them.'

The voice carries on.

One of the teachers shouts out, 'Excuse me but—'

'Shut up,' snaps Damian, and picks up his gun.

Lucas and Connor and Jase and Edison look at the screen. They gaze around the room, bewildered. They search for the row of black hooded figures. They look back at the screen. They recheck. They can't make it out.

The eyes of the Eternals turn to Damian.

'So what?' shrugs Damian. 'You kill kids, who cares?'

'Where d'you get it all?' says Markel suddenly. He gestures with his comm at the stash of guns, at the ammunition.

'None of your business,' repeats Damian, still smirking.

Markel looks like he's counting the guns, totting up the cost, trying to work out if having that many guns is normal. He stares up at the ceiling; a frown wrinkles up his face.

'*Who?*' he says to Damian. '*Who gave them you?*'

I flick my eyes to the Lock Down remote. It's still lying there on the mat beside the gun stash. I wonder if I can make the right move, in the right way, at the right moment. I wonder if I can bounce down and pick it up and smack my hand on the green button?

Damian turns back to Markel. His eyes are glittering. 'If I wanted to be asked stupid questions I'd have signed up for a quiz,' he says.

'*Who?*' demands Markel.

'And I think you've forgotten something,' continues Damian.

Markel is still staring at the guns, flicking his eyes to the pile of ammunition, glancing up at the ceiling, as if for the first time he realises he's caught up in something much bigger than Damian's Eternal Stupid Knights of Darkness.

'I gave you an order,' says Damian. His face is twitching. He's getting angry. He glances up at the ceiling too. 'And you'll do as I say.' He starts jabbing his finger in the air. 'When I say it.' He's not used to being challenged. 'Without a load of stupid questions.' He jabs his finger at Markel. 'That ain't your fricking business.' His voice is getting shrill. 'So do what I told you,' he snaps. 'You heard me. *SHOOT HER!*'

Markel looks at him.

'Oh, I'll shoot all right,' he says.

It's probably the longest sentence he's managed all day.

And he simply raises his arm, raises his gun, aims it at Damian and pulls the trigger.

# 6.35 p.m.
## Friday, 18 September

There's a gasp, a rolling echo of screaming cut short into terrified throats, a wave of kids pulling back, whimpering. And the dead silence of teachers.

Markel shrugs. He looks around like he just threw something in the trash. A strange smile hovers over his face. He likes killing, I can tell. It's there in that sinister, hovering smile. I see him again in weird flashback:

*. . . There are three of them. Markel lines them up against the bookcases. He yells, 'We gonna execute you.' He can't even say execute properly. He says, 'extra-cute you', like it's a deal on hair shampoo. He puts a bullet through each of their foreheads.*

*POW. POW. POW . . .*

Markel flicks off the news. He turns towards me.

I open my mouth to shout out something. But my mouth stays sagging open.

Because right behind Markel, something is moving.

Damian is twitching.

Damian ain't dead.

Markel raises his gun again. He plays with it like he's having fun, swinging it at me, swinging it away, snapping it back and taking aim at my chest.

And behind him Damian ain't dead. He's twitching his shoulder. It's gruesome. He's raising himself up, just a little, like he's doing some weird sort of a press-up. He looks dreadful. His front is drenched in blood. His guts, it must be his guts, maybe it's not his guts. But something ain't right about his stomach. I feel bad just looking at him. It makes you want to help him. Makes your stomach turn. And Markel carries on playing with me. My mouth drops open. There's so much blood. Slowly Damian drags himself around, drags his arm around.

He's got a gun.

A gasp goes up from the school. Markel chuckles like he's the original badman.

Damian's pointing his gun at Markel. I want to scream, to shout, 'Watch out!' Because Markel can't see Damian. It's just an instinct. To warn someone. To try to save them. But I don't.

Everybody's looking on in horror. Markel thinks they're doing that because of him, because he's the business. Damian raises himself on to one bloody elbow.

Damian struggles to align the gun. He struggles to get Markel in its sights.

And I still want to shout out. I want to say, 'Markel, behind you,' but I catch my words. I don't shout. I catch my voice and I swallow it. Because I know that if Markel gets shot, he can't kill me. And I want to live. I want to get out. And we'll all have a chance of getting out. I don't know what I'm hoping for. I can't bear what I'm hoping for.

I hold my voice. It rises up again in my throat. I hold it like a bubble in my mouth, a bubble that can burst at any moment. I don't know if it's right or if it's not. If I shout I can save Markel. If I don't shout maybe I can save myself, save the rest of us. But I don't know how I can just look on and watch a murder. Can you do that? Can you look on and do nothing? It feels like I ought to do something. It feels like all of this was because we all just stood by and did nothing, in the before time, in the time when we had every flipping day to sort out all the Connors and all the Jases and all the Lucases ever born. It feels like I'm watching a baby drowning in a bath and saying, 'I never put it there.' But Markel ain't no baby. And he's trying to kill me. So I just hold my voice in its bubble. I just watch. And I discover that I can. I can simply stand here and let it happen. And you know, I never thought I could do that.

Damian drags himself up a bit more. I wonder vaguely if he's strong enough. If he's going to die before he can make the shot. If I'm going to die before he does. He takes the gun in both his hands. He's rocking on his elbows. He looks terrible. His face is all twisted. He's not going to make it. The gun's wavering. He tries to steady it. Markel is smiling and smiling and swinging the gun. He's swinging it from me to some kids on the benches and he's started his little chant. 'Eeney meeney miney mo.' Markel's so damn sure of himself. Mr Big Man With A Gun. He's so damn sure he just snuffed Damian out.

Too damn sure.

Damian pulls the trigger.

There's a flash, not much of a flash. Markel deserved a bigger flash than that. Even a wannabe Big Man should've had a bigger boom. There's a bitter smell. The kids scream. Markel's down with that same surprised look I saw when Miss Carter fell.

His chest is a huge hole of raw meat. Blood jerks and spurts out, like the last major artery of the world just burst. A spray of blood hits the kids on the front benches, sprays across the trampoline, falls like spring rain on my face.

And my voice is still a bubble in my mouth, but it ain't

no good shouting anything out now, so I let the bubble pop. I watch the blood seeping over the Olympic-turf. I could have saved him. I knew I wasn't going to.

I watch as Damian slumps back down on the floor. Someone moves forward. Someone kicks the gun away from Damian's hand. Jase and Lucas and Connor and Edison and the ginger-haired boy exchange glances and their glances say: What the hell're we going to do now?

There's silence, like a void has opened up in the centre of the gym.

The Deputy Head is quick off the mark. She steps up and says in a loud, clear, commanding voice, 'Stay calm, everyone. Stay calm.' She turns to Connor and them, but there's no leader left, just stupid moronic Year Nines with guns.

Jase says, 'Shut up,' and waves the gun at her. He casts a look at Markel to make sure he said the right thing, but Markel is dead.

Lucas says, 'Yeah and sit down.'

The Deputy Head slowly sits down.

Then we all just stay there like that and there ain't no plan or nothing.

I know this is my chance. I know how Connor thinks, so I guess maybe the others are going to think like him too. So I say, '*PARLAY!*' again.

They like that. They like being asked permission to speak. They like to think they're still in some kind of computer game. They like to think they got ways of doing things, even if it's only the rules of some stupid, naff film.

'Leah wants to Parlay,' Jase says. Stating the obvious as ever. He looks at the Deputy Head like she's well rude, and didn't play by the rules at all.

'Thanks,' I say, taking that as permission. I notice Lucas may not be as stupid as I thought because he's bent down and fielded the Lock Down remote from Damian's mats.

I turn straight to him. I figure Jase is going to do what everyone else does, Connor ain't going to shoot me, the other two I don't know about, which probably means they're not players. But Lucas is holding the remote. He's holding it and looking at Connor. So who is the main man now?

Lucas or Connor?

# 6.43 p.m.
## Friday, 18 September

'Lucas,' I say, 'and Connor.' I keep it polite. They like that. 'I don't believe you guys signed up for all this.' I vaguely gesture at the bomb and Anton does me proud. He lights it up again in a pink and yellow strobe effect with his comm. 'If I could come up with a way to get you guys out, without no police and no Put-Up-Your-Hands-And-Spread-Your-Legs and no mum asking, Why? Why? Why? – maybe you'd listen.' I don't make that a question. I say it like it's already a statement of fact.

There's silence. At least there's silence. That means they're listening. 'This is all the fault of them people outside,' I say. I know they'll like that too. It says: You are so not to blame and this is so not your fault.

They do like it.

'Them people got more riding on a bad outcome to this siege than we know about,' I start.

Jase nods like he knows he is *so* everyone's victim, but I can see straight away that Lucas is not interested in

280

all that. The idea of going home appealed, but now I've lost him.

I change tack. 'Frankly, old sport,' I say, like I'm in a movie too. 'It's all getting a bit boring.'

'Yeah,' says Edison. 'And they never sent no pizzas.'

Beside me I can hear the whole school listening: the creak of bodies on the benches, the squeak of trainers on the boards, the rustle of a sweet being daringly unwrapped.

'So're we going to sit here till Monday?' I say. 'Or whenever they decide to blow us up?'

'Uh?' says Lucas.

Maybe I was wrong. Maybe he *is* stupid.

I change tack before my Parlay time gets finished.

'Miss Turnbull,' I say, talking now directly to the Deputy Head. 'If we can all get out alive, can you and the Senior Team agree to keep the matter of Lucas and Connor and Jase and them in-house?'

She squints at me like the idea is preposterous, like how could you possibly keep the matter 'in-house'.

'Yeah,' says Jase. 'I never did nothing.'

'Yeah,' adds the ginger-haired boy. His voice is full of it-wasn't-me whine.

I speak very slowly and clearly, because suddenly I see a way, and if I blow this I don't know what'll happen.

'Damian and Markel are dead,' I say. 'Miss Carter and

281

the rest of them are dead,' I say. 'But there's a lot of us who aren't, at least not yet. But, Miss, there's something that needs to survive in all of us more than just getting out of here.'

Miss Turnbull wasn't expecting that. She frowns at me. She's wondering what I got up my sleeve now.

I take a deep breath. I try to imagine I'm singing. I want my voice to have power. I want to find the right words. 'Miss, staff, students.' I pan my gaze across the school. I include the Eternals in my sweep. 'I think we need to be able to survive as human beings and still be able to trust one another.' I look Miss Turnbull straight in the eye. 'We need to be able to still see people as nice and stuff.'

She nods slightly, but mostly she's just looking plain confused.

Encouraged anyway, I continue. 'I don't know about you, Miss, but I only saw Markel killing people. And he's dead. I didn't see none of the other boys shoot anyone – even if they was carrying a gun.' Under my breath I say a silent sorry to Ruby. A huge, silent sorry, because it was Lucas who shot her, even though he didn't know it.

Miss Turnbull sucks in her breath. Everyone waits.

'I want you to lead the way, Miss, to show us how to be nice and stuff, show us how to forgive, so that, that thing in us what keeps us human, and keeps us trusting, will survive.'

'I see,' says Miss Turnbull. At least she's got some brains.

I underline it for her. '*I don't see anyone here, other than Markel and Damian, who shot anyone.*' I hold my breath. She's got to take the lead now. She's got to, or it's curtains for all of us.

The eyes of the school are on her. Their waiting hangs in the air. What will she say?

She don't say nothing, but I can see the authority in the gym has shifted. Lucas and Connor and all of the Eternal Knights are looking at her too, waiting for her to decide.

*And she still ain't saying nothing.*

'I don't know about you,' I say, hoping to persuade her more, 'but we kids hate them inspectors and people from outside coming in. We think you and the teachers should have the say.'

Miss Turnbull slowly nods her head.

'And we trust you,' I add with a new note. 'We trust that if you give us your word, you're going to keep it.'

'Who gets to keep what?' says Jase, like he don't get none of what's going on.

'I'd like to Parlay, please,' says Miss Turnbull. Her

283

voice is well humble, really sincere, even trembling.

Lucas raises his gun. Connor raises his. But Jase claps his hands, and Edison laughs.

'Please,' says Miss Turnbull.

I want to kiss her, because she's got it! She's figured out they need respect. She's going to bow down to them.

'OK,' says Lucas, 'you can Parlay.'

'I have a solution,' says Miss Turnbull. She struggles to say it, but she does. 'If you boys will put down your guns and allow us to leave, I will not be reporting your names to the authorities. I shall only be mentioning the names Markel Mcleod and Damian Phillips.' Her voice is wobbling. Her chin is wobbling. She don't like saying it, but she knows it's the only way.

Lucas gets it. 'Yeah,' he says. But I can't tell if his 'Yeah' means 'OK' or 'I understand'.

'What about them?' says Edison cunningly. He points at all the school, watching, listening.

Miss Turnbull turns and addresses the school. Her voice is quivering. 'Students and staff,' she says. 'We are negotiating a positive outcome to this siege. Anyone who does not agree to the terms I negotiate, will have to deal with me in my office. You are not to talk about this negotiation. If you do, you will not find anyone who will back you up. Do I make myself clear? Spreading false accusations is an offence and I for one won't tolerate it.'

There's a murmur from the kids. The teachers are looking at each other. I can tell straight the kids are ready to buy it; the teachers aren't. One Year Ten starts crying, sobbing, 'Anything anything.' No one says different. So the teachers are ready too – at least for now.

Miss Turnbull has factored that in too. She says, 'If anyone contradicts my version of events and wilfully and wantonly impeaches the character of any student during the days that follow our release, they might be surprised to find I am ready to go as far as to impeach them.'

It's a threat and not too veiled neither. In plain speaking: if you tell on Lucas or any of them, I will say you were also involved.

It feels like the whole gym is holding its breath. I'm holding mine. This is what I want. I don't care about the truth, or nothing. I don't want the stupid moronic politicians to win. I want us all to walk out of here. I want Miss Turnbull to prove what great students go to YOU OP. Students that can solve their own problems. Students that are not a threat to no one. I want the whole thing to backfire on the government. I want every news channel for the next week to be singing the praises of every YOU OP Academy, every YOU OP teacher, every YOU OP student.

I look at Lucas and Jase and Edison and Connor. They ain't looking too convinced.

'You mean, no charges?' asks Jase, like this is the first time he's considered he's done anything wrong.

'No charges,' says Miss Turnbull.

'And no rumours,' says Edison. 'No night-time nasty surprises?'

'No arrests. No vigilante groups. No accusations,' says Miss Turnbull.

Edison looks at his gun like he'd like to keep it as a souvenir.

'But you must put your weapons down,' says Miss Turnbull.

'OK, whatever,' says Edison, and just like that he quietly lays his AK-47 assault rifle down on the floor. He crosses over to the benches and sits down.

Jase looks at Lucas. The ginger-haired boy looks at Lucas.

Lucas looks at Connor.

So Connor is the leader now.

Connor don't move. He looks at me like I've somehow managed to spoil his fun all over again.

I step forward. I climb down off the trampoline. I'm not the same sister he left behind this morning. The same Leah who ran behind him cleaning up his mess. I'm not going to be his mug any more. I've been raised from the dead. I'm on borrowed time. This is life after death. I step right up to him. He raises the gun at me. 'I don't need you,' he says.

'I don't care,' I say. 'I'm not doing this to sort out your problems. I want to get out. I got a life and you are standing in the way of my future.' I raise my hand. He aims the gun. I can feel behind me the whole gym watching, holding their breath.

'Just stop being such a loser,' I say, 'and grow up.'

'You fricking grow up and stop following me around,' he snarls.

I don't mind him. I continue stepping forward.

'I don't need you, Leah,' he says. 'I don't need you to look after me.'

'Whatever,' I say. I'm only three paces away from him now.

'I can do stuff on my own.' He fingers the trigger. 'I'll kill you if I have to.'

'I still don't care,' I say. 'Live your bleeding, boring, pathetic little life . . .' and I stop. I just look at him. Is this what it's all about? Connor living his pathetic stupid little life?

'Is that it?' I look at him.

He looks back and his eyes are empty.

287

'Cons,' I say. I drop my voice. It cracks. It's laced with a sudden tenderness I didn't even know I felt. 'Cons,' I whisper. *'You've got a life; you've got a family, what's wrong with that?'*

He looks at me like he never thought he had nothing.

'I didn't know,' I say softly, but nobody can hear us. 'I was only looking out for you . . .'

'Because Mum can't,' he finishes sneeringly.

And I remember all the times I've said that, all the times I've bullied him and blamed him: *'because Mum can't.'*

I stop.

'No,' I say. 'Not because Mum can't, but because I *can* . . . I *can* look after you . . .'

And I realise that's the truth. I don't look after Connor or Sally because I *have* to. I do it because I can, because I *want* to. And that changes everything. 'I'm doing this, Cons,' I say, my voice squeaking, 'because you're my family, because . . .'

And I don't know this feeling that's hurting my chest. I never knew it was there. But it's the truth. All the hurting, all the anger is because deep down, under all the blaming, under everything, he's my brother.

He looks up at me. His eyes flicker, but he's looking at me, looking like he never ever considered that before.

'And I'm going to keep on looking out for you . . . even if you blow up the whole bleeding world . . . it's just one of those things, Con. I don't get to control it.'

'You don't control it?' he says puzzled.

He's still looking at me. Really looking, like he's seeing me for the first time.

'No,' I say. 'It controls me and that's all.'

And then I can see in his eyes that he's just a little kid, and he's reaching out for something. And it's been there all the time, but he's been believing it wasn't and he'd never find it. And he wants it to be there so much that he's ready to die for it. Die and take the whole school with him.

'C'mon Cons,' I croak. 'Let's go home.' I hold out my hand.

There's a slight pause. He blinks. Then shrugs.

Connor puts down the gun. He walks to Lucas. 'Give me the Lock Down, you dickhead,' he says. His voice is hoarse and rough, but it ain't unkind. Lucas looks at him and sees that he means it. He pulls out the remote and slings it at Connor.

'OK,' says Connor suddenly, like he's a new person, like he found whatever it was he was missing. He walks up to the Deputy Head. 'Here you are,' he says and shoves the remote at Miss Turnbull. Then he turns to the school at large and holds his hands in the air. 'Soz,' he says gruffly. And it's weird because how can you just say sorry after all this?

But the kids start cheering. One of them stands up and shouts, 'Go, Connor!' And suddenly they're all shouting, 'Go, Connor', like he's some kind of bleeding hero and never held no school up at all. He shrugs again and sits down on a bench by Edison and pulls out his comm and starts playing a game on it.

Miss Turnbull takes the Lock Down remote. She turns to the school and says in her hard, clear voice, 'Stay seated. We've been through a terrible ordeal; we don't want any more casualties. When you leave this place you should all remember what I said about not discussing the negotiations that took place here.' Her voice contains a clear note of warning. 'And we'll have an orderly exodus,' she says.

Then she presses the remote.

And she presses it again.

And she nods at Mr Doddwell to go and try the exit doors.

And Mr Doddwell clambers down from his bench as if his legs are well shaky. He hurries over to the fire exit. He pushes down on the fire bar and gets his shoulder well into the door.

290

And nothing.

Miss Turnbull goes over. She presses and presses the remote.

But nothing happens.

And we're trapped.

We're fricking trapped.

It's all been set up.

Some kids in the front benches start crying. Miss Turnbull looks worried. Her face has gone ashen grey. She hurries over to Lucas and Connor but I can tell from the shaking of heads that they don't have a clue about this.

Nobody does.

We're fricking well trapped.

# 7.00 p.m.
## Friday, 18 September

Mr Doddwell hurries round to all the doors on the gym, all the fire exits, all the external corridor routes. The only ones that are open are the internal access doors back on to B corridor.

Miss Turnbull looks at me.

I ain't got a clue what to say. Well, that's not entirely true. Maybe one clue.

I cross over to her. 'Miss,' I say. 'Please don't call the police. Please. I can't explain it. But I called the police before I dropped in on you all, and they didn't help.' I drop my voice. 'I think they got some stake in all this. I think they don't want us freed.'

Miss Turnbull looks at me like she thinks I am so berserk I must be mental plus ten. 'Leah,' she says, 'you've been wonderful, amazing, we owe everything to you, and don't think that I'm not grateful, but you've had a stressful day, a terrible day, and I can quite understand that you are imagining everyone is the enemy, that you aren't safe anywhere. Today has traumatised you.'

'No, it ain't that,' I say. 'Well, yes it *is* that, but not *like* that.' I don't get no further. The words I want to say don't come, and I'm left stammering there in front of her like a pre-school kid.

'And it goes without saying, I am very grateful to you for brokering the deal I've made with Lucas and Jason and Edison and Clive and your brother. It's not a deal I am happy to have entered into. I think you know that, but for the greater good . . . and with time . . . well . . . and then there was the bomb.'

She's speaking of it all in the past tense, like all that is already over. I want to scream: *Don't you see it's not over? The enemy never was Markel, nor Damian, nor the Eternals.* We haven't even started to sort out the real problem . . . but she cuts me short.

'We've had Damian on file for a long time. We know about his obsession with guns. We've been screening his visits to violent websites. The welfare officer assured us only last week he was not a threat. He was wrong. We were wrong. We knew nothing about him building bombs . . .'

'I don't think—' I start. But it's no use.

'It was the bomb that forced my hand. With Damian and Markel dead, we had no way of knowing if they'd set it on a timer and . . .' Here she stops. She looks worriedly up at the bomb.

'We really do need to evacuate the building VERY quickly,' she snaps. 'They may have set it to go off at any moment.'

'Miss,' I say frantically. But she's not listening.

'I will honour the deal as far as I can, but now I've got a lot of distressed children and frantic parents and I need to call out.'

'No!' I yell.

For answer she collects her comm from the cache in the ball basket and touches in a number. All the students start grabbing their comms too, trying to call out.

I run back to the centre of the gym. The students are all making one hell of a noise, but I cup my hands around my mouth and I shout up at Anton, 'JAM. UP. THE. AIR. WAVES.' I hope he hears me. I pray to God he hears me. I pray he can close the connections in time, because as sure as hell he ain't going to be quick enough to stop Miss Turnbull's call.

And as soon as Peterson knows we're getting out, he'll blow us up. He'll have to. He's in too deep. He's set to prove YOU OP kids are dangerous. He can't risk the truth getting out. Dead men tell no tales. I've worked it out. It's all about killing the kids.

Miss Turnbull is just saying, 'We've got the situation entirely under control. We want you to come and let us out. It appears Markel Mcleod and Damian Phillips have rigged a bomb to booby-trap us, and as you know Lock Down is a hundred per cent efficient at not only keeping rioters out but, it appears, keeping us in . . .'

Then she stops. She looks at her comm. She re-touches in the number. She puts it back to her ear. She shakes her head.

I give Anton the thumbs-up. 'How long have we got?' I yell up at him.

He scratches his head. He holds up one hand, fingers spread wide.

Five.

Five minutes.

# 7.07 p.m.
## Friday, 18 September

I've figured it. Lock Down, a hundred per cent efficient unless there's carbon dioxide. I race back to Miss Turnbull. I don't bother with 'no', 'please' and 'it's like this', or 'it's like that'. I grab a gun, that's all. It's easy. The guns that was causing so much trouble are just piled there on the front bleacher, and everyone's stepping round them like they're poison. I grab a gun. I grab all the guns. I walk right up to Miss Turnbull. I dump the guns at her feet. I hold the one I got up to her head. A deathly hush falls over the gym. 'I ain't got time to explain,' I say, 'but believe me, if you don't all do exactly as I say, I will put a bullet through Miss Turnbull's skull.'

I can see I got their attention.

'If you've picked up your cell comms,' I yell, 'put them back down now. If you got any other electrical thing put it down NOW!' I shriek.

The kids look at me like I've gone berserk, like I'm doing all this to mug them. Don't they realise the people outside can track every single one of those cells? Every game consul, every iPod?

'Line up,' I bark. There really is something in my voice like when I sing. It's got power. It's got authority. They know I am not kidding. And I'm not.

The kids stand and shuffle in a badly formed line into the centre of the gym.

'Connor,' I say, 'I need you to help me.'

He looks at me like I ain't never asked him for help ever before. 'Take a gun and get these kids to O wing to the tech corridor to the farthest point away from here – you hear? Line them up by the exit.'

He nods. He snatches up another gun.

'And do it fast.'

He nods and points to the first line of kids. 'Get moving,' he says. The kids nearly fall over themselves running to get out on to B corridor.

'I'm going to stay here with Miss Turnbull until you've got them all there. If anyone gives you nonsense, shoot them. Try not to kill them, a finger, hand, arm, anything – but get them to hurry.'

Connor nods.

'I'm going to catch you up,' I say. 'I'll send Miss Turnbull first, then Anton and me are going to come next.'

'Leah,' he says, like he knows something bad is going to happen.

'Anton's jamming the airwaves but he can't hold it longer than 'bout five minutes. When the bomb goes, the carbon dioxide content in the air will trigger the release on Lock Down. It's automatic. It will override anything from outside done to keep the place secure. There will be enough carbon dioxide to trigger every goddamn Lock Down in the bleeding country.' I laugh. 'Get everyone out of the building and then put the gun down.'

'I get you,' he says.

'If I don't make it,' I say, 'Aliesha's in the air vents above the science wing. Get her help once you're out.'

He nods.

'Get going,' I say.

'Leah . . .' Connor looks at me like he just found something and doesn't ever want to lose it again.

'Yeah,' I say. 'I know.'

'Make it home, Lee,' he says.

And he's gone.

I wait there with Miss.

The gym empties. Connor makes them move really fast. I see little Tilda Strickland leave. I pray to God she makes it home. I pray to God her mum gets her back.

As the last kid goes, I turn to Miss. 'I'm sorry,' I say,

'but I didn't have time to convince you. As soon as Anton can't keep the airwaves jammed any longer, they're going to blow the place. I know you don't believe me. I hardly believe myself.'

She looks at me, baffled.

'Do you hear me?' I say. 'They're going to blow the whole gym up.'

'But,' she says. 'Surely? Who?'

'Yes,' I say. 'They will. They're trying to do it right now. It's only me and Anton and Connor who are stopping them.'

'But,' she says again.

I look at her. I shake my head.

'And this gun,' I say. 'Which I don't need no more.'

I throw down the gun. 'Get moving, Miss,' I whisper. 'Wait by the Lock Down on O wing down by the tech corridor; catch them up. Run. Run fast. When it goes, you'll be out of here.'

'But, Leah,' she says, 'what about you?'

'I'm waiting for Anton,' I say. 'We got our own deal. He can't move because he's the one jamming the signals. If he loses it for a second . . .'

But she looks like she's going to start again. 'Hey,' I say. 'Get the kids out and don't forget the deal with the Eternals. Make sure they don't close down YOU OP 78 for no stupid reason. Make sure they don't win.'

She nods. She's getting the picture.

'We need this school. We ain't got money for no Free Schools nor Public Schools. We need our school. You hear me? It's ours. It's our school.'

She leaves and I don't have to threaten her with no gun.

All of them are gone.

'Lee,' says Anton into the quiet of the gym. I look at all the empty benches, the line of cell comms still giving off their signals, still lying on the seats.

'Ant,' I say. 'I reckon they'll check we haven't moved location before they blow. They'll tune into these cells. They'll think the kids are all still sitting in here snug as a bug, then they'll detonate.'

'Yep, probably,' he says. 'Get going, Lee. You need to go now.'

'Uh-uh,' I say. 'Not without you, Ant. We got a deal.'

He looks puzzled.

'I got to survive and I got to do it my way. Remember?'

'You're crazy,' he says.

'My kind of survival just ain't about Number One,' I mutter.

He pauses. 'Lee,' he says hoarsely. 'Leah Jackson.'

I blush.

'You really are crazy.'

'Probably.' I smile.

We look at each other across the dim spaces of the empty gym.

'C'mon, we did it,' I say.

'You did it,' he says.

'And we're going to live to tell the tale,' I say. 'Ant, as soon as you lose the signal, jump down.'

I run to the trampoline. I start shunting it, dragging it, heaving it, into the centre of the gym. 'Jump, Ant, you hear?'

'Yep,' he says, his voice echoing oddly off the brick walls.

'We'll take it at a run,' I say.

'We won't make it to humanities,' he says.

'I know.'

'And I don't reckon much for our chances if the blast catches up on the open Crossing.'

'We'll sprint. Get up to A corridor and back up into the science wing, down as far as we can go. There's more walls there, what with all the tech dens, more cushioning from the blast,' I say.

'OK,' he muses. 'It might help.'

'We can do it,' I say. 'We can make it to where it all started: Lab One.'

He laughs.

'If we make it,' I say, 'we'll get Ali out with us.'

'Yeah,' he says. 'Good plan.'

'We can do it,' I say.

'OK. I can't hold the signal any more,' says Anton.

This is it.

He jumps. I imagine all the spiders' threads around him snapping.

Suddenly he is right beside me. 'Run,' he hisses.

I leap from the gym, burst through the door, don't bother with nothing else; I'm on to the corridor like a bullet. I pull at corners and bins and swerve the lockers. Chairs and all crash to the floor. I tear through everything, swerve everything, rip through air like it's got a sell-by date.

Footsteps crash behind me. Anton? Must be Anton. Clever Anton.

I can hear ragged breath right at my back. Someone's bellowing.

'Since Connor gave the remote to Miss, the comm's been on live feed,' Anton yells. 'I left it filming in the gym, relaying it straight to Victoria. They won't get away with it.'

Clever Anton.

Up ahead is the first lab. When I reach it, I see ten

empty metres, like a marathon stretching ahead. Just do it. Just make it through. My leg's bleeding again. I weave in between the lab benches, ducking, leaping, twisting.

The windows start rattling. They're small, thick things, made of cheap blast-proof plastic, suitable for our kind of school. They mask another sound, something booming. I tilt my head, trying to make it out.

But I know what it is.

It's coming from the gym.

# The
# After
# Time

SATURDAY, 19 SEPTEMBER

## Injuries and Deaths in the YOU OP 78 School Siege

**Miss Maria H. Carter, age 47,**
killed by gunshot wounds to the head.

**Aliesha Mulholland, age 16,**
shot in the face.

**Theo Harvaskio, age 12,**
killed by gunshot wounds to the head.

**Carmen Murawski**
sustained minor injuries from the splintering of a desk she was hiding under.

**Dunelda Timms, age 11,**
shot in the arm.

**Felixia King, age 11,**
killed by a shot between the eyes.

**Steven Finbow, age 11,**
killed by a shot between the eyes.

**Tracy Snoops, age 11,**
killed by a shot between the eyes.

**Miss Olivia Fish, age 28,**
killed by multiple gun shot wounds to the head, and chest and neck.

**Miss Judith Turnbull, age 44,**
Deputy Head, minor injuries to the back.
**Nathanial Durrel, age 12,**
shot in the knee.
**Yusef Ali, age 15,**
shot in the back.
**Ahmed Safi, age 15,**
shot in the shoulder and neck.
**Brandon Farquar, age 14,**
killed by a shot to the head.
**Ruby Krysler, age 11,**
killed by shots to the hand and chest.
**Damian Phillips, age 14,**
killed by a shot to the abdomen.
**Markel Mcleod, age 15,**
killed by a gun shot wound in the chest.
**Anton Evans, age 16,**
killed by multiple blast wounds to the head, chest
and lower body.
**Leah Jackson, age 16,**
killed by multiple blast wounds to the head, chest
and lower body.

# Acknowledgements

I'd like to thank:

**Nigel Baines**
**Sakky Barnor**
**Beverley Birch**
**Susie Day**
**Ruth Eastham**
**Sophie Hicks**
**Caroline Johnson**
**Gill Quarcoopome**
**Naomi Pottesman**
**And everyone at Hodder Children's Books**

Thank you so much for all your input and support for SIEGE.